BELLS IN AN EMPTY TOWN

'Black Heart' Crowle thought he had Logantown tamed, till a drunken horse-thief named Harve Gould raised the wind again. Crowle threw Harve in jail but he knew his brothers would get him out, but the brothers died. So almost, did Marshal Amos Crowle, pinned out to broil under the desert sun, a stake for his black heart.

He was saved by a fancy younker called Rainey Jay. But Rainey was a member of the Jonquil Gang and they wanted to take Logantown, pillage it and rape it. The town emptied, while church-bells tolled and survivors fought to the death in the hot and dusty street.

BELLS IN AN EMPTY TOWN

BELLS IN AN EMPTY TOWN

by
VIC J. HANSON

MAGNA PRINT BOOKS
Long Preston, North Yorkshire,
England.

British Library Cataloguing in Publication Data.

Hanson, Vic J.
  Bells in an empty town.
  I. Title
  823'.914(F)   PR6058.A59/

  ISBN 0-86009-598-3

First Published in Great Britain by Robert Hale Ltd, 1979

Photoset in Great Britain by
Dermar Phototypesetting Co, Long Preston, North Yorkshire.

Printed and bound in Great Britain by
Redwood Burn Limited, Trowbridge, Wiltshire.

CHAPTER 1

Horse-thief Harve Gould was pretty drunk. He was glad to sleep it off in the town gaol. His brothers would get him out come morning he said.

Drunk, Harve had been waspishly affable and Marshal Crowle's task hadn't been hard. But Harve's two brothers, poison-toads both, were a different proposition altogether.

The town waited, holding its breath in the heat and the dust. And, finally the brothers arrived. They braced the marshal on main street and the elder one, Burt, said, 'We want Harve.'

Marshal Crowle said: 'You'll have to go through me to get him.'

It was as simple as that. There was no more talking. The brothers walked for-

7

ward. They fanned out, making a wide gap between them. Crowle didn't move at all at first; he stood with long arms dangling at his sides, his shoulders bent forward a little almost as if he had a natural stoop, which he hadn't: he was a straight lean man who wore only one gun, a forty-four calibre Dragoon Colt six-shooter with an eleven inch barrel, custom-built, precision-made, a famous gun carried by a notorious man. He didn't wear it too low and its holster wasn't tied down, the exceptional length of the weapon's barrel keeping it snug to his thigh.

The youngest Gould brother, Kimmy was a sort of Fancy Dan. With his neat dark clothes and bright red checkered kerchief he wore twin pearl-handled shooters low-slung on his trim hips above black tooled-leather riding boots. Older brother Burt, older even than jail-bait Harve, was, like the marshal, no kind of dresser at all. Rumpled duds that looked as if they'd been climbed into. Shapeless hat. Single battered Frontier model Colt. Of the two, the marshal had at least had a shave this morning. But he certainly wasn't one to go on appearances. He was a deliberate man with a dark lean face, with hooded eyes and a thin sardonic smile. But he wasn't by any manner of means a procrastinating or particularly slow-moving character, just relaxed was all, like a rattlesnake in the sun.

It was he, in fact, who took the initiative. 'What're we waitin' for, boys,' he said and suddenly he wasn't where he had been in the first place. He had moved sideways from the position he had first held. Then there was a sort of *flurry* of action and violence and noise and the gunshots echoed and re-echoed along the street and, it seemed way off into the hills beyond, then rolling back again as if rebounding.

Fancy Kimmy fired only one shot and the slug ploughed into the ground. Kimmy hadn't been as fast as he looked.

The marshal fired all of three times, maybe four. There was quite a lot of smoke, and some dust too. The marshal had not only moved sideways but had gone down on one knee also; but now he was slowly rising. Kimmy Gould had managed to pull only one of his pearl-handled shooters. He lay flat on his back in the dust as it settled slowly. His fancy black hat lay near him and the thin trickle of bloody seeping from beneath his head looked black too in the brilliant sun. One bullet had got him in the shoulder, spinning him around; the other had drilled his temple.

The older brother, Burt, was still on his feet, although he had dropped his gun. He staggered sideways, tottering, tumbling finally to the hoof-pocked ground, becoming still. Marshal Crowle had been creased in the fleshy part of his left shoulder. No bones had been touched. He holstered his gun, walked forward. A cursory glance at Kimmy and Burt Gould was all that was

10

needed. Here now were two harmless hunks of dead meat and that was the end of it. Disregarding people who aimed to help him along, Crowle turned and walked back towards his office. But his friend old Doc Lessiter was soon bumbling along after him calling:

'Amos!'

Pint-size Rab Gray the undertaker was inspecting the corpses ...

Amos Crowle was a legendary character, a gunfighter supreme and, up till right now things had been pretty quiet in Logantown since he took up his post there. Many of the hard-hats had moved on. Others stayed. But, for the time anyway they sang small. The previous marshal had been shot in the back by a drunken swamper who was subsequently discovered out on the range, his neck busted, a stolen horse limping nearby.

When such a lowdown breed as a saloon swamper started to get hornery it was time to take notice: the goodfolk

11

of Logantown didn't want another "open town", another hellhole.

It had cost them plenty to hire the man known tò owlhooters the length and breadth of the wide Southwest as Black Heart Crowle. Maybe then, with things so all-fired quiet again they had begun to regret their decision and the dinero that went with it. But horse-thief Harve and his brothers changed things again ...

After the shoot-up Amos Crowle was around town for three days with his arm in the sling that Doc Lessiter had insisted he wore; then he took the sling off and decided to escort Harve Gould to the county seat for trial. He had a dodger on Harve, who was much more than a mere horse thief. Like his brothers had been, he was wanted for murder and highway robbery. Crowle left his deputy Jake Philpott in charge during his absence. Jake had been out of town on a small legal errand when the Kimmy and Burt shoot-out took place.

The journey took the marshal and his prisoner across a wide area of arid badlands. There was no waterhole in the whole stretch so they went supplied with extra canteens, brimming full.

There was a frenetic quality about Harve Gould's jauntiness now. It was obvious that the violently-induced demise of his two brothers had hit him pretty hard. The last of a lawless clan, the three had been mighty close.

It was early when the two men started out but there were already indications that it was going to be another scorching day. A few people were already abroad. Harve waved to acquaintances as the marshal led him out. There were only surreptitious glances in return. Friends Harve had, but they were all in bed. Only suckers got up this early.

There was a lot of dust and the two riders were soon out of sight of Logan-town. They travelled at a steady walk-ing-trot which ate up the miles, bringing Harve ever nearer to the inevitable hang-rope.

The outcrop of bald boulders, like misshapen eggs in an immensity of sand and useless rock, stood approximately in the middle of the badlands. They were in more ways than one a landmark. If travellers across this arid waste gained this point still intact and not too thirsty, and with water to spare, they had a prime chance of reaching the other side.

The sun was at its zenith when Harve Gould and Amos Crowle reached Buzzard Point, as this outcrop of bald rocks was known. 'We'll rest in the shade,' the marshal said. 'It's about goddam time,' said Harve. They dismounted. To be on the safe side, Crowle had his shooter in his fist.

Three riders came out from the other side of the rocks.

Crowle found three guns levelled at him. Two Colts. And one double-barrelled sawn-off shotgun.

'Drop it, marshal,' said a man.

Crowle shrugged and dropped it.

* * * *

If Harve Gould had anybody at all who was as close to him as his brothers had been it was Seth Bancroft. Seth was born in the same Arizona town as the brothers, and he and Harve, who was of about the same age, had been boyhood pards.

For a time Seth had been a member of the Gould gang. But Seth had not got on well with the oldest brother, Burt and a split had come. Seth still kept in touch with his old boyhood chum, Harve, however, and recently their paths had crossed again in Logantown. Marshal Crowle knew Seth Bancroft as a hardhat but it was doubtful if he knew of Seth's former close ties with the Goulds and, in particular with the fun-loving Harve who, of all the clan, best got on with the rest of the populance.

It was a welcome surprise to Harve

to meet up with old pard, Seth, in the shadow of Buzzard Point. And Seth had two of his hard-hat friends with him and all three of them were armed to the ears.

Amos Crowle did not reveal his surprise or his chagrin. His dark poker-face remained set. 'Hallo, Seth—Brock—Joe,' he said. 'You boys must have left town mighty early.'

'We did, Amos,' said Seth Bancroft. 'We did.' He had hair like straw and an engaging grin. 'Shall I plug him, Harve?' he asked.

'Untie me first,' growled Harve.

The man called Brock sliced Harve's bonds with a Bowie knife and all four men watched as Harve rubbed his wrists vigorously, cursing as the circulation returned.

'You're a cruel bastard, Amos,' he said. He held out a hand to the man called Joe. 'Give me your gun.'

Joe handed it over and Harve levelled it at Crowle.

'Put one in his gut,' said Seth.

Harve cocked his gun, his eyes slits, beads of sweat running slowly down his face.

Slowly, he let his hand fall, until the gun was hanging, heavy.

'No,' he said in a choked voice. 'That's too easy. Let's peg him out in the sun. Away from here. Out there in the waste off the usual trail.' He waved his free hand. 'Out there where no-body'll find.'

Amos Crowle flung himself at Harve who was so completely taken by surprise that he did not have time to press the trigger, thumb the hammer, raise the gun or swing it or anything.

He went down with Crowle atop of him, Crowle's one hand at his wrist, trying to wrest the gun from him. The other hand was at his throat.

The fingers were like steel talons. Harve began to choke. Then suddenly the grip lessened and Crowle's whole dead weight fell upon him.

Seth had slugged the marshal on the

back of the head with the barrel of a gun.

Crowle came to his senses with the sound of retreating horses in his ears, the soft beat slowly dying until finally he could only hear the whispering sand.

They had stripped him. Already the sun's rays were uncomfortable on his bare flesh and its rays beat like copper hammers on his unprotected and misused head.

They had done their job well. He was flat on his back, his arms drawn out in an agonised stretch above his head, the wrists lashed with rawhide, maybe the very same piece he had used on Harve. This then was tied to an improvised stake, which he could not see. But he could feel it and it seemed as immoveable as deeply-imbedded rock. His legs were lashed in a similar way and attached to a twisted shrug with a thick rubbery stem that looked as if it had been there for centuries. This arid landscape was a primitive one.

Crowle pulled, wriggled. There was no give at top or bottom, none at all: he was stretched as if on a rack.

He was off the beaten track—and even the usual trail, passing by Buzzard Point was not used greatly. Those hellions had fixed him up like a scraped porker for roasting. He cursed obscenely for a few moments before realising that he was just wasting much-needed breath. He began to fight again savagely, his teeth gritted, his eyes tightly closed.

He did not seem to be making any progress at all. His head was a huge balloon of pain ... But it would not float away. One of those bastards had given it a hell of a crack. He would have throttled Harve Gould otherwise. Maniac laughter bubbled in him. They were long gone now. But he would bet Harve's gizzard was still sore. The laughter bubbled up inside him and then came out in little spurts. His skull now felt as if it was full of holes all filled with redhot coals.

He kept himself supine now. The hot agony beat at him ...

He must have passed out after all, he didn't know; he was floating, no need to fight anymore. But something inside him would not let him be, would not let him give in. And the sun was not so hot now, he thought. Maybe it was waning.

There was a shadow, a cloud perhaps; was there a freak storm brewing after all, breaking in on the long drought? The badlands: they were all drought! He was part of that drought, a husk. He was lightheaded. His head to one side as far as he could force it, he slowly, agonisingly opened his eyes.

After a bit he saw black, dust-caked riding boots which looked new beneath the dust and were decorated by a pair of large wicked-looking Mexican-type spurs.

The shadow over the sun was the shadow of a man.

A canteen was held to Crowle's lips and a deep voice said in a drawling conversational tone, 'The buzzards attracted me.'

Water trickling down his chin, Crowle tried to laugh. 'They don't waste much time, do they?'

'No. I reckon they thought you were dead meat. I did too, at first. They hadn't touched you yet I guess but they were getting pretty close, waiting at the ringside kind of.' The man moved; he cut the bonds at Crowle's wrists and feet.

The tall, lean naked man groaned aloud as he laboriously bent his knees, his elbows. He began to curse in a sardonic monotone and his rescuer said, 'You've got quite a vocabulary there, pardner. I didn't think there were any wild Injuns left in this territory.'

'This ain't Injun work, friend.'

CHAPTER 2

His name, he said, was Rainey Jay Dodson.

He said he had heard of Marshal Crowle. His voice gave nothing away and neither did his smiling eyes. Crowle did not ask him why he had such a strange moniker—if it *was* his own. It took imagination to think up a name like that one.

He was young, younger than Crowle. He was darker than Crowle, as if maybe he had some Indian blood in him. He spoke pure American, though, spoke it better than Crowle did. He was dressed fancily. Like Kimmy Gould used to dress, Crowle thought.

'Let's get over to the rocks,' said this handsome, fancy young stranger. 'We'll try to get you some covering somehow.'

Crowle walked awkwardly. His body was sorely red and he felt as if he was slowly burning up. Fortunately the sun was going down at last and the horizon was purple.

They sat in the shadows of the bald rocks that made up Buzzard Point. Rainey Jay Dodson produced a threadbare but clean pair of pants which fitted Crowle not badly at all. Also a spare rough blanket in which he cut a hole through which the marshal's head fitted. He wore the blanket like a poncho and looked like a Mexican peon. But then, on top of this a large red and white spotted handkerchief around his head gave him a gypsy look, a strange mixture.

Dodson laughed, white teeth gleaming in the dark face. He had the look of the devil about him. 'No shoes I'm afraid, marshal. Not even mocassins.'

Crowle's feet felt like slabs of raw meat. 'Some rag mebbe, so's I can wrap 'em.'

'Yeh.' Dodson produced an old war-bag that looked as if it had been used for wiping down a horse. He cut this into two pieces and Crowle managed to fasten them to his feet with some pigging string that the younker also produced and slashed in half with his large claspknife. During all this time Dodson's horse, a handsome little paint stood watching them with intelligent eyes.

Then, with dramatic suddenness the beast jerked its head up in a listening attitude.

'Something's coming,' said Dodson and he caught the paint's reins and pulled her further into cover.

Peering through gaps in the outcrop of round boulders, the two men watched the approaching riders. Four men on four horses. And one riderless horse besides.

Oh, my achin' head an' bleary eyes, thought Crowle, *it can't be!* The riderless horse looked like his own! Maybe the whole thing was a sort of mirage.

But the mirage did not go away. It became clearer and clearer. Harve, Seth, Brock and Joe were returning!

Crowle did not reason why. 'Lend me a gun,' he said to Rainey Jay Dodson.

The younger man handed over his spare gun, a battered but serviceable forty-five with a cut-down barrel.

'Need any help?'

Crowle shook his head slowly from side to side and Dodson smiled his flashing smile and said no more.

The riders veered away before they reached the rocks. They were obviously making for the spot where they had pegged-out the marshal. They began to slow down, leaning forward in their saddles, peering, wondering no doubt whether they had made a mistake. They were still in range, though, and Dodson said, 'You could pick 'em off from here. Want to borrow my rifle?'

He was a very helpful cuss. And an unquestioning one too.

'No, thanks,' said Crowle.

He raised one hand and shaded his aching eyes. The four riders had split apart, one of them leading Crowle's horse. One of the others shouted and they all came together again and then they dismounted. They had found the spot they sought, the cut ropes. One of them, it looked like Harve, got down on one knee, something long in his hand—a long stake, or a pole.

They began to move back, nearer in fact to Buzzard Point, their horses trailing behind them. Crowle started to go out from the rocks and Dodson halted him with a hand on his arm, which the taller, older man tried to shake off.

'Take the other gun, you'll mebbe need it.'

Crowle took the second gun then. He nodded his thanks, his sombre red-rimmed eyes lit momentarily with the same kind of sardonic devilry that lurked in Dodson's own.

Like a walking scarecrow Crowle hobbled out into the open, into the fading red glow and the lengthening shadows, a strange figure, like something from a dream, a scarecrow half-Mexican and half-gypsy, its long shadow moving blackly like a spectre before it, the guns hanging loosely at the end of the long arms: all squiggly black patterns on the sand.

One of the guns had a longer barrel than the other and that lent another bizzarre and dreamlike touch.

And the four men had seen him now, were facing him, the one with a stake— and it *was* Harve—holding it in front of him like a lance.

Crowle flopped suddenly, stiffly onto one knee and pointed the two guns, the poncho fanning out as he raised his arms like bats'wings. Pointing the guns all the length of his long arms as he started shooting.

One man went down flat as if he had

been kicked by a mule but the others started to shoot back and Crowle was rolling, the slugs cutting up the dust around him. A horse screamed in agony and went down. Two other horses broke away, men on their backs low over the saddles, holding on hard, not getting chances to do any more shooting. They had been taken completely by surprise. It would have been hard to determine their feelings, whether they were yet aware that they only had one man against them: he might have had a small army hidden in the rocks, this magician who had escaped from rawhide and the killing sun.

Crowle raised himself on both knees and fired his guns rapidly, but the horses went madly on, their riders clinging.

Rainey Jay Dodson ran to his own mount and got the rifle out of the saddle boot. Vision was not good now. He took two potshots at the fleeing horseman, cursing, knowing he had missed.

Rifle in hand, he went out from the rocks towards the marshal who was on his feet again, his back to Dodson, the two guns held in front of him as he moved forward again, a flapping scarecrow figure. Another of the horses broke away, galloped away. One man lay still. Another stood facing Crowle, hands empty, stood swaying from side to side, knees bending, empty hand raising now as he clutched himself, then pitching forward, down, twisting, lying.

Crowle reached the fallen man and stood looking down at him. He was still moving slightly. Crowle got down on one knee, placing his guns carefully on the sand behind him, out of the wounded man's reach. He picked something up and Dodson, reaching him saw that it was a straight bough that had been whittled to a wicked white point at one end.

Dodson veered away a bit and took a cursory glance at the man who was motionless. He had had the life ripped

29

from him. Dodson returned to the marshal who had risen, dropped the stake, picked up the two guns again. But then he went down on one knee again, holding the guns. 'Why did you come back, Seth?'

'Gimme a drink, Amos,' whispered the young man with hair like dried yellow straw.

'You've got a slug in your gut,' said Crowle.

'What the hell ...!' Seth started to cough, bright blood running from the corners of his mouth and frothing over his chin.

Dodson whistled the paint and she came over and he got his canteen and handed it down to Crowle who put it to the dying man's lips. But he only took a spot and then he began to cough again, violently, covering his front with shining blood. Taking the canteen back Dodson grimaced at the mess on its neck and wiped it vigorously on his sleeve. He leaned over now beside Crowle as the dying man began to talk in little coughing, grunting spurts.

'Harve was eaten up ... His brothers ... He thought you might get away after all. We tried to tell him, me an' Brock an' Joe but he wanted ... He came ...'

A further spasm of coughing interrupted the halting near-incoherent narrative. Seth reached out a hand, clawlike and gripped the cloth of Crowle's borrowed pants, a handful, clutching it, holding on.

'Harve, he made that stake. He—he was goin' to drive it through your belly.'

Crowle said, 'You did yourself a bad turn, Seth, you an' Brock an' Joe, when you decided to put in with Harve.'

'Yeh.' Seth coughed again. It sounded like a laugh. 'Amos ... the others ...?'

'Brock's dead. Joe and Harve got away.'

'Was Harve ...?'

'Harve seemed to be all in one piece, Seth. But I'll get him, make no mistake about that.'

'Yeh, get my friend, Harve ... Amos ... I ...'

The coughing laughter started again. Seth was still laughing, coughing, when he died.

Crowle rose to his feet. 'Injuns would've made a better job of the whole thing,' he said sardonically and he turned about and began to weave his way back to Buzzard Point.

His rags had been scuffed off and he was barefoot again. The kerchief tied to his head had fallen lopsidedly over one ear.

His improvised poncho remained intact. He looked not unlike a huge grounded bat, and a drunken one at that.

He weaved in a rough half-circle and then came back to Rainey Jay Dodson.

'That's my horse,' he said, pointing.

He wandered around until he found his own gun too, the special Dragoon Colt. Seth had had it, had dropped it. Crowle inspected it, blew into the barrel. He said: 'I'm kind of attached to this iron.'

Dodson said. 'It's certainly some gun.'

* * * *

Harve and Joe finally quietened their fractious horses and slowed them to a jog-trot.

Harve said: 'We should've stopped. There was only two of 'em.'

Joe said: 'The hosses bolted didn't they? It all happened so sudden. Brock went down. He was a goner all right. I guess they got Seth too. Or they've taken him in. Who would've expected Crowle to come at us like that? That other feller must've cut him loose. Who was it? Was it somebody from town?'

'No, don't think so. Looked like a stranger.'

'Crowle had the luck. Hell, I'll say he did!'

'He ain't gonna get away with it. I'm

goin' back.'

'You please yourself, Harve. I'm gettin' outa this territory altogether. I ain't aimin' to get in any goddam war with Amos Crowle.'

Harve squinted. 'I'll go back into the hills. Jonquil and his boys are there. I'll wait.'

'I know Jonquil's in the hills. But I ain't aiming to get mixed-up with that loco Mex again either ... No, I've got connections.' Joe's voice became suddenly boastful. 'I'm gonna be long gone, Harve.'

Harve began to slow his horse. 'Well, like I said, I'm going back.'

'Suit yourself.' Joe stopped his horse and Harve halted his own mount and Joe stuck out his hand and Harve clasped it and they shook.

'Take care, Harve.'

'Sure.'

Harve watched the other man ride away.

Joe did not look back.

Harve would never see him again. Nor would Marshal Amos Crowle or anybody else connected with Logantown. One of Joe's "connections"— maybe the only one—was an ex-mistress of his who ran a whorehouse in Prescott. She had, of course, gotten herself a new man who objected most strongly to Joe's reappearance and countered Joe's threats and demands with a bullet in the face from a derringer, killing him stone dead ...

After leaving Joe that day, Harve Gould acted as if he aimed to return directly to Logantown. He, at least, went someway in that direction. But he actually skirted the town by miles and made for the hills beyond. Logantown was roughly bounded by the badlands on one side; and on the other, after a span of fairly lush rangeland, dried-up though it now was, there was an area of low, sprawling hills and narrow, perilous canyons.

As Harve left the badlands at one

point, Rainey Jay Dodson and Amos Crowle were quitting them at another and making directly for Logantown. The marshal, lurching in the saddle a bit was astride his own horse.

They had left the corpses near Buzzard Point to the tearing mercies of the obscene birds that gave that area its name. They could not have toted the bodies anyway.

As well as being half-fried, Amos Crowle was murderously tired and he knew he must get fixed up and rested before he took up Harve Gould's trail once more, although he had no doubt he would do this eventually. That Harve! Him and his pointed stake! Crowle began to wish he had kept the stake. He would certainly know what to do with it when he caught up with Harve. He began to chuckle as he rode. Maybe all that sun had turned him a mite loco. But there were lots of folks thought he was loco already, so what the hell!

Having an idea that his companion was looking at him strangely, he tried to quell his mirth and, eventually he succeeded in quietening himself down. He had not yet made up his mind about Rainey Dodson. Correction: Rainey *Jay* Dodson! There was a name to conjure with and no mistake.

The fancy young gink had certainly saved the marshal's bacon—he owed him!

CHAPTER 3

The Jonquil gang was camped in a green hollow in the hills where there was a small pool.

They comprised a half-dozen all told, with Jonquil (Jonni for short) at their head, making up the six. Nobody knew whether Jonquil had another name. He was a Mexican who had moved over the border about six years ago with a small band, only two of which now remained, so that the present six were split evenly between Mexicans (or *mestizos*) and Norte-Americanos.

Felipe was on watch that night when he heard hooves clattering over the rocks. Felipe wore mocassins, as each man did when on guard: Jonquil was a good general. Felipe slipped over the rocks and waited and then moved out into the narrow cutting, his rifle pointing at the newcomer. The man halted his steed, was clearly seen in the starlight.

'It's me. Harve Gould.'

'Why didn't you whistle, Harve?'

'I didn't know whether I was being followed. A crazy lawman an' another feller. I think mebbe I shook 'em off but I didn't want to take any chances. I know how Jonni likes to protect this hideout.'

'All right. Come ahead.'

Felipe, on foot delivered the rider to the hollow where the small fire burned, its flames reflected in the pool. Then Felipe returned to his post. Harve's welcome was cheerful and noisy, until somebody asked about his brothers and he divulged what had happened. Then the boys were suitably grieved, the Mexicans making a more sorrowful job of this than their more phlegmatic gringo pards.

The three Gould brothers had often joined the Jonquil gang in their depredations on both sides of the border, as also had Harve's boyhood friend, Seth Bancroft and his two pards, Brock and Joe.

Harve could not be perfectly sure whether Seth and Brock were dead or not. But he now opined to the others that Crowle would have finished them off. Harve explained how he had wanted to drive a stake through Crowle's belly. Jonquil thought that was very funny. He was a big, lithe, middleaged man with curly black moustachios and long black hair with a broad band of white across the crown where, in his younger days an Apache had tried to split it down the middle with a war-hatchet. He hooted with laughter now, showing all his large yellow teeth.

'You should've made sure of him in the first place, amigo,' he said, spluttering. 'You should've sliced off his eyelids so his eyeballs would fry. You should've cut off his *cojones* an' opened up his belly an' stuffed 'em inside.'

'I ain't had all the practice you've had, Joni,' put in Harve, this remark sending the bandit leader off into further uproar.

They squatted on their haunches round the fire and sipped coffee, and Jonquil, his mirth finally quelled, became silent. Maybe Logantown would be worth a visit. Up till now, following the old adage that a dog doesn't shit on its own doorstep, Jonquil had never led the gang into a job in, or near Logantown. For another thing, one side of that particular town was bounded by the badlands (the original settlers must have been simple or fatalistic or something) so that the gang on their way out would have to take to the hills almost directly, and Jonquil didn't want anybody ferreting for him here.

He liked this hideout, with its almost fresh water, its shelter from surprise attack, its close proximity to the Rio Grande and the Mexican border. From here he had led his men on sorties far afield in Arizona, New Mexico and Texas, as well as back over the border, never failing to shake off pursuers before going to ground here in this, his favourite bolthole.

Here in this little hollow too, when the weather was bad, they could pitch tents beneath a convenient overhang with water only a few yards away and room for the horses.

Seemed like Harve was reading Jonni's mind; his mouth full of tortilla and beans which one of the men had fixed for him Harve now said, 'We ought to go in an' take that burg apart.'

'What for?' asked Jonni. 'For fun?'

'Take the town over, I mean,' said Harve, his eyes shining in the firelight with pride at his own brainwork. 'Suck it dry. It's been done before. Quantrell did it.'

'I ain't fighting no war, amigo.'

'Rich pickings, though, Jonni. Rich pickings. The bank. The stores. The saloons and other such places ...'

Harve let out a sudden guffaw, peppering the fire with sizzling beans. 'Some tasty young wimminfolk too.'

'Yeh, yeh,' said one of the Americans, a yellow-featured poisonous character called Yank Brady.

'I'll sleep on it,' said Jonni, passing Harve a bottle of tequila.

Harve was happier now. He was not the sort to mourn for long, though he still aimed to get Amos Crowle somehow and avenge the deaths of his brothers, Kimmy and Burt. By the time Felipe came down from the lookout, his place being taken by Yank Brady, Harve was deep in a drunken sleep and snoring mightily.

Everybody else was down too, and Felipe, after drinking the dregs of the coffee and cursing softly over cold tortillas and beans rolled himself near to his chief.

'Did you tell Harve about the new gringo we got comin' Jonni?'

'No. He should be here now.'

'Mebbe he called in at Logantown.'

'If he did perhaps he'll be able to tell us more about the place and its new marshal.'

Jonquil had heard about Amos Crowle but had never seen him.

Jonquil reflected that any man who could blaze down Burt and Kimmy Gould—and Seth and Brock too maybe—must be some hombre. Jonquil drifted off to sleep thinking that he would like to meet face to face with this gringo hell-hound they called Black Heart Crowle.

Lily Duboissier was young and very beautiful. She came originally from New Orleans where her father was crippled by a gambler who ran off with Lily's mother. When her father eventually died, Lily left New Orleans. She had the same restless temperament as her mother; she liked men too ... And her father had left her money.

By the time Amos Crowle arrived in Logantown, Madam Lily Duboissier's Café in the French Style was the premier eating house there, better than the hotel dining room, either of the three saloons or of course the various hash-houses and cantinas.

The new marshal began to eat there, and to sample Lily's good wines, which she had delivered by waggon from time to time, strapped down and sealed in special cooling containers.

At this time Lily had no regular beau, though previously she had been courted by a rancher named Sam Prentiss, a middleaged widower with two growing boys.

She was a prize to be coverted, a jewel in a weatherbeaten wasteland, and Sam coverted her greatly. Not so his sons, however, dull boys who had been very attached to their dour and ugly mother and still had not gotten over her loss, taken away by hard work, disease and lack of expert medical attention two summers before. And Lily would never have made a rancher's wife anyway, particularly on a small tooth-and-nail spread like Sam Prentiss's. So the affair died a slow but definite death and Sam was seen only rarely in town, a doleful taciturn man once more, just the way he had been in the old days.

So, when Amos Crowle arrived in Logantown, Lily Duboissier was once more ripe for a liaision with a well-set-up mature man. She had had her fill of boys. And Crowle had a reputation as a ladykiller as well as an executioner of men; he was never the backward sort.

After Crowle's ordeal in the badlands, Lily was one of the people who saw him ride in with Rainey Jay Dodson, by darkness now, as she took the air on her front stoop.

Although she had not been awake that early, she knew that Amos had left that morning with his prisoner, Harve

Gould on their way to the county seat. She was certain sure that Amos had not been hatless at the time and clad in a blanket, *serape, poncho* or whatever that baggy unprepossessing garment was. And the man on the paint pony who rode beside him now was certainly not Harve Gould, was younger and much better-dressed than Harve had ever been, making Amos look like some kind of outlandish scarecrow.

She waited a while and then, holding her skirts up against the dust went down the street to the marshal's office. A few people greeted her, all men, except for one Mexican *puta* on the prowl. Lily answered them all in her friendly way. The men did not presume, as one or the other of them would later presume on the senorita. Respectable womenfolk did not usually walk the streets alone at night, but Miss Lily was an exception. She made her own rules, went her own way like a beautiful, unapproachable, dangerous cat.

Besides—it was said she favoured Marshal Crowle. And no man wanted his head blown off, even for a delectable creature like Lily Duboissier.

As Lily reached the office-door it opened and the young man who had accompanied Amos came out. He doffed his hat and gave her a slight bow, unspeaking. Then he went to his horse and, before closing the door Lily looked back to see the young man leading the pretty paint pony down the street. He turned his head and she saw the flash of his teeth and she closed the door behind her. Deputy Jake Philpott was in the office and, as usual when coming face to face with Lily he became inarticulate and pigeontoed. He did manage, however, to convey to her the fact that the marshal was in the back room.

Crowle lay on his back on the bunk, naked. 'My,' said Lily. She looked him over. 'Have you sent for Doc Lessiter?'

'Nope.'

'You certainly need something.' She went to the door and called Jake and asked him to go back to the French Café for her. He was glad to do this. He returned with some special salve with which Lily laved the marshal's misused body. Soon he was covered all over with cream-coloured grease and gleaming under the lamplight. Though a lean man he was a muscular one and laughing, Lily said, 'You look like a sunbaked Greek god.'

He grabbed her, taking her by surprise. She hadn't realised he had so much strength left in him. As he pulled her down she said, 'Wait a minute, Amos. You're getting that stuff all over my clothes.'

He let her go and quickly she undressed and joined him again, let herself gently down upon him.

* * * *

The town committee or council or

whatever they called themselves wanted to see Crowle later on the following day. According to Doc, who carried the message, they had had a meeting last night but had thought the marshal was not fit enough to attend. Horse-shit, Crowle thought; Doc was just being diplomatic. Because Doc had asked him, he'd go today though. Hell, he was all right; mite sun-dried was all.

As Doc left, Deputy Jake Philpott came in. He was younger than Crowle and taller, a gangling look about him. He had been deputy to the previous marshal, the one who got himself shot in the spine by a drunken swamper. When Crowle arrived Jake had elected to stay on. There was a shy, deceptive quietness about him. He did not scare easily and he was good with a gun.

There was a wary friendliness between these two men.

Jake was a dutiful cuss. If he were marshal he would trot to the committee every time one of them whistled. But

Crowle did not hold this against him. He thought he could depend on Jake if the chips were down.

'Make some coffee, Jake,' he said.

'Sure, Amos.'

Crowle smiled sardonically as Jake hastened to do his bidding.

Busying himself with pot and cups, the deputy said over his shoulder, 'That Rainey feller who came in with you last night, Amos, I just saw him ride out. Did he come in an' see you an' say so-long?'

'Nope. Mebbe he was just going for a constitutional. Which way was he heading?'

'Towards the hills.'

'Wal, anyway, he was under no obligation to me. The other way round in fact. Besides, I guess Mistuh Rainey Jay Dodson ain't one for such frills like sayin' so-long an' that sort o' thing.'

'Yeh, I guess you're right.' Sitting drinking coffee the marshal became silent and Jake let him be.

Crowle wondered whether Rainey Jay Dodson would return to Logantown or whether he was fiddlefooting on to other pastures in the manner of his kind. Crowle understood that kind, as he was by way of being of that kind himself. He wondered idly whether he would ever see Dodson again; then he dismissed the younker from his mind.

Some time later he wandered down to Lily's place for his midday meal which he took today with the proprietess herself as company in the back parlour.

Afterwards he got out his "makings" and made himself a smoke. He leaned back in his chair with his belt loosened and wreathed himself in a blue cloud. Lily sniffed. She herself favoured long, thin faintly-perfumed cheroots.

After kissing her in an almost husbandly way, Amos meandered off to the town meeting.

It was in the church as usual and he handed his gun to the verger as he entered. He still had a derringer tucked into the back of his pants, hidden by his scuffed leather vest which he had donned for the occasion.

The elders were all present. In his chequered career Crowle had seen a good many bunches like them. There was Doc, who came forward to greet him. Doc was all right. So was bearlike Cal Lippton, the liveryman who was the next to shake his hand and ask him how he was.

'Sore,' said Crowle and did not add to this statement.

There was paunchy banker Ephriam Saunders, booming a false greeting. He was all right as bankers went, but his little eyes never seemed to look at a man straight. Although probably the richest man in Logantown he seemed strangely insecure. Maybe his wife had something to do with this. Crowle had been present, among other town dignitaries, members of this present bunch for instance, at one of Trudy Saunders' "Dinner Parties". She was a plump, fancy little redhead, younger than her husband. Crowle had wondered what she would be like in bed.

There was Kit Blaine, the mayor, a vague round man with a white blob of a face, who let himself be pushed from all sides but never committed himself, exasperated everybody. Kit no doubt had his uses. But how, for Pete's sake, had he ever got to be mayor in the first place? Maybe it was just his turn.

There was Rab Gray, the pint-sized undertaker, Bud Juleson who owned a couple of stores, rancher Rollo Earle, who Crowle had only met once before; there was Jerry Rand who kept the Silver Horseman Saloon ...

The pack, thought Crowle. Yes, he had seen plenty like them in too many other towns like this one. They had sent for him. They had hired him. And, if they felt like it they would pull him down ...

Preacher Soames was there, a long length of droning sanctimoneousness, eyes like a timber wolf with colic. Given half a chance he would be the first of the pack to show his teeth, and quote the Word of God in justification.

The only absentee, as far as Crowle could see was loud-mouthed Jack Trisket, who owned a haulage business ... Jack did arrive. But by this time Crowle was finishing his report to men lolling in pews, and none of them lolling more than the marshal himself.

The only man standing was Preacher Soames and he was demanding that a Christian burial should be given to those poor lost souls out in the desert. He was talking about Seth Bancroft and his pal, Brock, out there in the badlands, buzzard-bait by Buzzard Point.

'Hell, they're dead ain't they?' said liveryman Cal Lippton.

Amos Crowle's sentiments exactly.

Still, those bodies were sort of proof, in the absence of the only witness, the young man Dodson, that the marshal had done what he'd said he had done.

'Here's Jack,' said Ephraim Saunders. 'I guess he'll supply a waggon.'

'A waggon for what?' said Trisket and they told him.

The burly, cantankerous man was surprisingly cooperative. 'I'll go an' see one's got ready,' he said and bustled away again.

CHAPTER 4

It was twilight when Rainey Jay Dodson reached the hills. He had taken his time, stopping for leisurely chow and coffee on the way, over a small fire he lit by a cluster of rocks. His trailing was just as leisurely—devious too—when he came to the foothills. After a while he left his horse, then he took his boots off. He walked pigeon-toed like an Apache scout. The Mex on watch had no awareness of anything until the cold barrel of a Colt was pressed to his neck.

'All right, amigo. Take me to Jonni.'

Jonni was uproarious.

Harve Gould was not so happy though. 'This is the stranger who was with Crowle,' he said. 'He took a shot at me an' Joe. I seed him.'

'Go back to your post, Juan,' spluttered the bandit leader. 'And don't let any Injuns creep up on you.'

The crestfallen lookout gathered up his gear and, with an enigmatic glance at the newcomer stole away into the night.

Rainey Dodson and Harve Gould stood facing each other, Harve bristling like a cat, the other man totally still, totally relaxed. The others clustered round as Jonquil spoke the new gringo's name. Dodson did not offer his hand to anybody.

'I'm part-Injun,' he said conversationally as he lowered himself to a seated position on the ground and began to put on his boots, which until then he had carried in his hand. He made no explanation to Harve. And Harve, after his first outburst stood sullen, holding his body stiffly, crooked, in a *puzzled* sort of attitude.

Jonquil said, 'Here's one part-Injun gringo that Juan won't forget in a hurry.' He started to laugh again and, in between spasms handed Dobson an uncorked bottle of tequila.

Dodson took a deep swig and blew out his breath. Then he said, 'You got something lined-up, amigo?'

'Possibilities, amigo. Plenty possibilities.'

'You always were a cagey bastard.'

'My sainted mother always said so!' Jonquil began to laugh again.

'You're also the laughingest man I ever did see,' said Dodson, and that only made things worse.

Harve Gould muttered a curse and left the light of the small fire and went and lay down in his blankets.

'Harve's gone to bed early,' spluttered Jonquil. 'He ain't a laughing-kind man nohow.'

None of the rest of the gang had met Dodson before, but he and Jonquil were old friends. Jonni, never one for secrets, told how that had come about, and even Harve left his bedroll again and crept forth to listen.

'Just a keed, this hombre way,' said the bandit leader. 'But *macho,* much *macho* I tell you. He was on the run from the Rurales and had had his horse shot from under him an' he limped into the hacienda of my old friend, José Lanolito. You remember José, Felipe?'

'I remember José,' said Felipe, who was Jonni's oldest compadre there. But Rainey Jay Dodson, or whatever he called himself was before even Felipe's time.

'José hid him from the Rurales,' Jonni went on. 'And he stayed at the rancho. When the border wars began we fought side by side. Then Rainey, that was hees only name then, said he wanted to see more of America ...'

'I've been getting myself a sort of education,' said Dodson.

'I can imagine,' said Jonni, and he went on: 'We ran into each other in Sante Fé three weeks ago when I went up there alone, you boys remember, to see a feller who owed me money ...'

'He saw the feller,' put in Dodson.

Jonni jerked a thumb. 'I saw Rainey too, an' it was a better meeting.'

'For me too. Particularly as I didn't finish up dead like the other feller.'

'I got my money. We met, jest by accident. We celebrated. We arranged this meeting, for this very day.' Jonquil threw out his arms. 'And here he is. I knew he'd be here before the night was out. I did not give heem up. And I might have known he would not come een like anybody else.'

'Like Harve did,' said Felipe maliciously. 'At the business end of my rifle.'

'Sure.' Jonquil guffawed. 'Sure!'

'I couldn't get here earlier,' said Dodson. 'Like maybe last week for instance. I told you.'

'You told me. And did your business in Sante Fé get satisfactorily concluded?'

'I had to wait. But, yeh, it got

concluded.'

'Another drink?' Jonquil handed over the bottle. They hunkered down—all of them except the disgruntled Harve who returned to his bed once more.

'What happened to José Lanolito?' Dodson wanted to know. And Jonni said: 'He died een bed like all good men. The holdings are handled now by José's nephew, Esteban. You don't know heem.'

'What's he like?' said Dodson.

'We do business now an' then,' said Jonni, non-committally.

'Keed,' he went on. 'You never told me why you were running away from the Rurales on that day.'

'You never asked me. Neither did José if it comes to that. I went with a girl. She was a plant. Her and her boyfriend rolled me, took everything I had. They almost killed me, but not quite. When I was well again I tried 'em down. I used a knife, just the way they did. With the man, quick. With the girl, slow. But I didn't muffle her good and she squealed like a little pig ...' Dodson shrugged, spread his hands.

Jonquil laughed. The others laughed.

There were now eight men at the hideout. Three Mexicans, counting Jonquil himself, and five Norte-Americanos. Juan and Felipe were the only two remnants of the original gang that had come over the border with their leader. Two had gotten themselves killed. Three had gone back, had lost touch, might even be dead too, or in gaol. Their places had been taken—partly—by three Americans. Big untalkative Pat Grimson. Small redbearded ''Fox'' Raymond. And the lean yellow-faced Yankee called ''Yank'' Brady, a fugitive from the stews of New York.

They all rubbed along all right, as long as they were planning or knew something was in the offing. They were all a bit edgy at the moment because they had been at the hideout longer than usual and there was not much room to move about. Jonquil did not like them riding out: he guarded this particular bolthole with jealous cunning.

Harve's visit and the news he had brought had created a diversion; and now here was Rainey Jay Dodson. There was animation again, laughter—some of it at the expense of poor old Harve.

Harve was back in his blankets. And now Juan came down from lookout and Fox Raymond took his place. Juan went to his bedroll and, one by one the others followed his example, except Jonquil and Dodson, who sat by the small fire a while, talking sofly. Their heads were close together, two blackhaired heads, like Indians, Jonquil's with that white slash across its crown.

'You and Marshal Crowle, tell me about it.'

Dodson told him the whole story. Grinning, Jonquil listened him out but this time did not laugh out loud.

And, when Dodson had finished

Jonni said, 'Keed, I have a proposition for you.'

* * * *

'He's back,' said Jake Philpott.
'Who?'
'That Rainey feller.'
'Oh.'
'Did you expect him back, Amos?'
Crowle shrugged. 'Where is he?'
'In the saloon.'
'Make some coffee, Jake.'
'Sure, Amos.'
Coffee was drunk, cups and pot were washed and put away; and Jake had gone out for a while on a duty pasear when Dodson came into the office.
'Morning, Amos.'
'Mornin', Rainey.'
Dodson waved a lean brown hand. 'There ain't much out that way. Just hills, river, border.'
'Yeh.'
'I thought I'd go over the river. Then

I thought, what the hell! Lot o' stinkin' little Mex towns. Dust and heat. Hotter than here even.'

'Yeh.'

'So I came back.'

'You on the run, Rainey?'

'Nope.'

'We just finished coffee.'

'I had a drink, thanks. I saw Jake.'

'A good man, Jake, better'n he looks.'

'Yeh, appearances are kinda deceptive sometimes. Did you know I'd left town, Amos?'

'Yes.'

'Yeh, you would wouldn't you? It's a nice town. I'm a fiddlefoot, but I guess I've got to settle sometime, if only for a while. I didn't know whether to keep riding or not. Then I remembered I hadn't seen you again before I left.'

'You don't owe me anything, Rainey. It's the other way round.'

'You'd have done the same for me.'

'Yeh.'

'You need another deputy, Amos?'

'I dunno. Mebbe I do. But I don't think the town council 'ud stand still for the cost.'

'It was just a thought.'

'I'll let you know.'

That noon the bodies of Seth Bancroft and his pard, Brock were being put under the sod, what was left of them: the voracious buzzards had worked fast. Rab Gray's arts were of little use. Stronger-gutted townsfolk stood in line to view the bodies at the funeral parlour.

Quite a crowd followed the hearse to the graveside and nobody even cracked a smile at Preacher Soames' sonorities. Neither the marshal or his deputy were present but the stranger called Dodson was. He did not speak to anybody, though, and he did not join in the post-funeral festivities at the Silver Horseman. Later, somebody said they thought they had seen him go into Pearly Jane's crib on the edge of Mextown.

Jane and two other girls hung out there.

In the middle of that night a late-drifting reveller heard screams coming from Pearly Jane's place and because he was full of Dutch he went over there.

The light was on and the door was unlocked and he opened it and then the light went out and something exploded in his face.

Dawn was breaking when a very sober drunk came to his senses. He could hear something moving. And then the naked girl wriggled across the floor to him. It was Pearly Jane and she had been beaten very badly; cut with something sharp too by the look of her.

The man yelled for help and folks came along and, after a bit the marshal, Amos Crowle himself. The reveller was as sober now as he had ever been in his life but he had a headache worse than any hangover and a lump on the side of his head. Even so, Crowle was pretty rough with him before finally letting him go. He had not seen who had hit him, had not seen anybody except the girl who now lay moaning on the couch with Doc Lessiter ministering to her.

Crowle went over. 'She tell you anything?'

'She says she didn't know who it was. It was too dark.'

Crowle jerked a thumb. 'That galoot said the light was on before he opened the door.'

Jake Philpott had arrived and now called out: 'Here are Jane's two friends, marshal.'

Crowle went back. He scowled at the two fillies. 'Where've you been?'

'What's the matter with Jane? What happened to her?' It was the smallest of the two, a little plump half-breed who spoke.

'She's bein' taken care of. I asked you a question, miss.'

The other girl answered. Slatternly-looking; puggy face and a lot of brittle yellow hair; some Swede about her. 'We had a date. Both of us. Together.'

'All night?'

'Yes.'

'So Jane was on her own?'

'Yes.'

'Did Jane have an assignation with anybody?'

The half-breed decided to put her oar in. 'Not that we know.'

And the slatternly blonded shook her head vigorously.

'She's dead, Amos,' said Doc Lessiter from behind them and the two girls broke into wild lamentations.

Nothng wails like a whore, thought Crowle cruelly.

They left—the marshal, his deputy, the doctor. The only one needed there now was Rab Gray. Crowle had the names of the two men who had been entertained last night by the half-breed and the Swede. Two middle-aged, respectable townsfolk. They had hired a room from an old Mexican biddy and the four of them had had themselves a time there. Crowle would take delight in questioning the two, seeing them squirm in their fat guts. He figured the girls were telling the truth all right.

Doc Lessiter said, 'I think she was lying first off about not knowing who it was. Then I think she suddenly realised she was going to die and she tried to tell me something. But she could only croak. I couldn't make out a word. I think he meant to kill her outright at the finish. Maybe he thought he had. He was interrupted. Apart from the other bruises and wounds her throat was partially slit, Amos. It's a miracle she lasted as long as she did.'

Crowle thought: *Whores!* They usually came to some kind of a bad end out here—particularly the unprotected freelances like Pearly Jane and her two friends.

He had heard that Pearly was in a house in San Antonio before she came to Logantown. Well, some of those city critturs, if they saved their money and got out before they wore out managed to make a life for themselves. Pearly Jane had been kind of long in the tooth for one of her ilk though. She'd gone way down in the scales of whoredom.

The story was that she had put her money into pearls. She had worn them too, and that was how she had lost them: this was not the first time Jane had gotten herself beaten up, but this time it was for keeps. Had one of her old San Antonio paramours caught up with her? It hardly seemed likely. What had Jane had left that anybody would have wanted except her worn-out body, and that had been getting cheaper day by day, from day to day, from long night to long night!

'A drink?'

'Sure,' said Doc.

'Sure,' said Jake.

They went into the Silver Horseman Saloon and were greeted by landlord Jerry Rand, a fast-looking man with a thick black moustache.

Rainey Jay Dodson was playing cards

with three other men. He saluted. Over their drinks, leaning against the bar Crowle said quietly to Doc, 'Dodson asked me for a job as deppity.'

Jake Philpott scowled. It was the first he had heard of it. Doc said, 'What did you tell him?'

'Nothin'.'

'The committee wouldn't go for it, not a second deputy. Besides, you're not exactly their blue-eyed boy right now.'

'I know. I did mention the committee, now I come to think of it.'

'A young hellion,' mused Doc.

'Yeh.'

'Yes, I know you're no pantywaist an' we wouldn't have got you here in the first place if you were. But you're a professional lawman with a formidable reputation. Who knows what your friend Rainey actually is?'

'I wouldn't exactly call him a friend of mine, even if he did save my life. I guess I do owe him something though.'

'We could put it to the committee.

But, even if they consider him we'd need to ask him a lot of questions.'

'I don't think he's the kind of gink who would stand still for questions,' put in Jake Philpott softly.

Crowle did not seem to be listening anymore. By now Jake had become accustomed to his superior's moods. He called Jerry Rand and asked him if he could fix him up with a meal. Jerry reeled off about half-a-dozen basic examples and Jake made his choice. Doc said it was time he got home for a meal too, or his housekeeper, Minnie would have his scalp.

The idea of motherly silver-haired Minnie with anybody's scalp was amusing and Jake sniggered. Crowle made no sign he had heard the remark. But when Doc said, 'So long' the marshal replied. Then he said to his deputy, 'I'll go down to the office an' wait for you. Then I'll go to Lily's place.'

'All right, Amos, I won't be long.'

CHAPTER 5

Later, when Crowle got back from chow at Lily's, Jake had the two whores waiting at the office, the little half-breed and the yellow-haired Swede.

Jake's shy approach had totally disarmed them. They just were not used to shy men. Crowle questioned them again, more gently this time. But they had no more information of use to give to him. They both said that Pearly Jane had been alone when they left her, that she had not had a visitor before that, none of them had, it had been a bad evening. And Jane had not mentioned any other particular visitor who might call later. Jane had no particular favourites and sometimes men just came without prior arrangement.

Neither of the girls had seen anybody lurking near the cabin when they left it last night. Crowle let them go before they got too tearful again; their tears made him savage.

'Do you think they'll be all right?' said Jake.

'Whadyuh mean, that that maniac with a knife might have a go at them now?'

'Yes.'

'I hardly think so. And neither of us can spend time guarding 'em.'

'Mebbe you do need another deppity at that,' said Jake.

Crowle looked at him with a thin smile playing about his lips but did not say anything. And, grinning, Jake went on, 'You gonna check with those two townsmen or shall I?'

'We'll lock the office up and we'll go right now and we'll take one apiece.'

'And I can guess the one you've chosen.'

Crowle chuckled mirthlessly. 'The

girls said they were with them all night. Let's see what *they* say. C'mon.'

Ten minutes later Crowle was sitting in the back office of the freight station run by Jack Trisket and Trisket faced him across the other side of a big scarred desk.

'I tell you the bitches are lying, both of 'em,' Trisket blustered.

'Wal, Jack,' said Crowle, 'I'm not here to judge you. I'd be the last one to do that. I like the flesh o' wimmin as good as the next man an' better'n most. I just want to make sure that the girls were where they say they were. I don't want to think that those two did the job on Jane themselves, though it's possible. I've seen worse things in cat-houses when those fillies have a feud going.'

'I tell you, Amos, they're lying. I was home with my wife all night. She ain't well.'

'I might have to confirm your story with her.'

Trisket lurched to his feet. 'You've no right ...'

'Sit down, Jack.'

Trisket sat down again, his face losing some of its crimson as he looked into Crowle's dark stony eyes.

'You did know the girls though, Jack?'

'Sure. Who didn't? You ain't been here long, Amos.' There was a hint of patronage in Trisket's tones now. 'So you don't remember when those three girls almost got themselves run out of town.'

'No. Tell me.'

'Pearly Jane was here first. She came to work in Mama Boola's house in Mextown. The half-breed and the Swede turned up later. The three of 'em teamed up and split off on their own and took that cabin. Up till then Mama Boola hadn't had any competition, except mebbe for occasional floaters. Mama took a bunch o' the others and they tried to burn down that cabin. Pearly Jane

78

came out with a shotgun and cut loose, set 'em running, peppered a few asses.'

Crowle smiled. Trisket went on:

'Wal, that wasn't good for business. Mama Boola's business that is. Mack Julius was marshal here then and 'twas said he kinda fancied Pearly Jane. She wasn't so beat-up then an' she was right sprightly. Anyway, Mack smoothed things over, said there was room for two places in town or somep'n like that. As long as they kept themselves out on the edges, y'know!'

'Yeh. What happened to Mack Julius?'

'He went on a trip to Kansas City to see his old Maw who was dying. He was knifed and robbed there.' Trisket's face went a mite redder. 'In a cathouse! They never caught the feller who did it. He was one o' the pimps. He lit out, taking three of the girls with him. Incidentally, I just heard recently that Mack's old Maw got well an' she's still alive. Must be about ninety I guess ...'

Trisket's voice tailed off. Crowle was watching him quizzically, head tilted a little to one side. 'Let's not get too far from the subject at hand, Jack. I'm sorry to hear that your missus ain't too well. But this is a murder case—whore or no whore. I've got to investigate all possibilities. I'll have to check with your missus.'

'All right, Amos.' Trisket slumped lower in his seat. Suddenly, too, he was not the loud-mouthed blustering Jack that Logantown knew so well. He looked tired and old. 'I'll admit it. I was with the Swede. My missus had taken a sleeping draught—but she heard me comin' in early this morning and I told her I'd been out of town. I don't know whether she believed me or not. We— we ain't got the married life we used to have, Amos. I don't want to hurt her though.' He waved a large hand. 'If it wasn't for her I wouldn't have this business, wouldn't even be here maybe, could be fiddlefooting anyplace, sleepin' in cribs with harlots a damsight worse than the Swede maybe.'

'Why didn't you tell me in the first place?'

'Oh, I dunno.' Trisket's face reddened again and, with some of his old bluster he said loudly, 'Mebbe I don't like being pushed.'

'All right, Jack. Incidentally, right now my deputy should be questioning your—er—other colleague of last night.'

'I've no comment to make on that.'

'I wonder if he'll try an' cover for you.'

'Makes no difference now does it?'

'No, I guess not.' Crowle rose abruptly. 'See yuh, Jack.'

'Amos.'

You never can tell about people, thought the marshal as he went back down main street to his office.

According to Jake, the other fellow, unlike blustering Jack Trisket, had twisted and turned like an oily snake.

Which was what he was after all; and Crowle for one couldn't help preferring loudmouthed Jack.

Thaddeus Rainbow was not, like Jack Trisket, a member of the town council, but, because he was such a pious little cuss and a friend of Preacher Soames, he had been asked to sit in a few times, particularly when Church doings were under review.

Thaddeus was a widower with one daughter of marriageable age that no man wanted to marry: she was too much like her old man in build, features and manner. Between them they ran a feed-store with vinegary efficiency, cash on the barrelhead always, and charges for delivery worked out on mileage.

'I approached him gently,' said Jake. 'You know me, Amos.'

'Yeh.'

'An' he tried to high-hat me an' I didn't like that. I said I'd bring the half-breed, an' the Swede too, down to the stores. That sourpuss daughter of his'n wouldn't of liked that.'

'That was quite a ploy. Jake, my son, you're getting to be a man after my own heart.'

'Nice of you to say so, Amos ... Wal, anyway, he went down then like a popped pigskin.'

'No, he wouldn't want his straitlaced whelp to know he'd been a naughty boy would he?'

'He named Jack Trisket too, said him an' Jack were with the two girls all night.'

'It was a helluva hot night too,' said Crowle.

* * * *

After a succession of broiling days it was night when the storm finally broke.

First of all a heat, an even *greater* heat which came in off the badlands like deep gusts of a monster's breath; and it was followed by the wind and this too was hot, sweeping through the town and out the other side and whipping the grass of the range, all the time with a marrow-breaking sound.

Surcease from the heat did come at last. But surcease from the heat was no consolation at all for what followed. Rain became part of the wind, the whole thing now almost of hurricane intensity. Cold driving rain that stung like buck-shot and a wind that could drive a man off his feet, lift him, throw him.

People took shelter, bolted their doors, shuttered their windows. There were terrifying bangs and crashes as loose things became looser or completely detached from their moorings, flying through the air like missiles or demented birds thrown by the wind. Debris from gimcrack Mextown rolled and flew and skittered down Main Street. A man could get killed out there! So no man ventured abroad. He brought in his beasts and tried to quieten them.

However, the storm after all didn't last as long as many oldtimers had predicted, saying it was the "wuss" they'd ever seen. It was over by the following noon. But it had raised a whole lot of hell in its passing.

So maybe it was the "wuss" after all: the townsfolk could have been forgiven for thinking so as they licked their wounds. It was a mercy, they said, that so far no fatal human injuries had been reported; except a little drummer, recently in town, killed in his gig out on the range, his head on a rock.

Undertaker Rab Gray's pet pig had been killed by a flying fence-post. One of Cal Lippton's horses had suffered a broken leg and had had to be shot. But it was the damage to property that shocked people most. The town looked as if a horde of destructive giants had been on the rampage through it. Deputy Jake Philpott opined that, although this one hadn't lasted so long it had been more of a heller than the one he remembered a few years ago. And he was backed up on this by other townsfolk, boring the britches off "new-come furriners" like Amos Crowle.

'Mextown's a mess,' said a horseman, returning from there after searching for his pet hound-dog who had lit out during the hubbub. 'Flattened almos'.' He hadn't found his dog.

Debris was deep in Main Street. Including, among more mundane items an inverted dog kennel, a torn parasol that nobody claimed, a pair of ladies' long drawers with a split seam, a couple of buckets and a broken barrel, a privy door with a hole in it ...

A small battered ploughshare, claimed later by hostler Cal Lippton was found embedded in the left batwing of the Silver Horseman. And, most sorrowful of all was the fact that the lath and daub roof of the schoolhouse had been carried away, taking parts of the walls with it too.

Rainy Jay Dodson had taken a room over the Silver Horseman and played cards a lot there in the bar-room, ingratiating himself with the regular barflies and the people there who lived on the fringes of lawlessness. The rest of the time, unscathed, he wandered around town and, of the other establishments favoured particularly Madam Lily's Café, having his meals there. During the storm minor injuries had become commonplace and now folks demonstrated cuts and bruises and complained of aching limbs, but only in an offhand way in case other folks thought that they were just making excuses to get out of helping with the newly-organised rebuilding of the schoolhouse roof.

Amos Crowle went to visit Lily Duboissier at the Café in the French Style. One of the waitresses told him the proprietress was upstairs. He was at the top of the stairs when Rainey Jay Dodson came along the landing towards him. Lily's room was round the corner at the other end. There was a flicker of surprise in Dodson's eyes, and then they became hooded again and the lean dark face wore its usual inscrutable expression.

'Amos.'

'Rainey.'

Lily's door was closed, as it invariably was. The marshal rapped sharply on it with his knuckles but then without more hesitation turned the knob, opened the door, walked in. Lily, clad only in a white chemise, turned around at her dressing table where she had been combing her long raven hair. Her red lips were half open as if she were about to call out and she held an ornate comb lifted in her hand. Stones in the handle of the comb flashed as they caught the sun coming through the window, though the curtains were partially closed.

Lily's lips looked full, bruised. Her face was flushed, her eyes heavy-lidded. She had the appearance of a langorous cat who had just had her fill of something nice. Her eyes widened now.

'Amos. Hallo.'

'Hallo, Lily. I came along to see if everything was all right here.'

'Everything's pretty fair, Amos, thanks. One of the door's got to be fixed and we have a smashed window. One of the girls got cut by flying glass but she'll be all right.' The voice tailed off. Every curvaceous line of the woman's body was tense. Crowle looked at her levelly, no expression on his face at all, and he didn't come away from the door which still stood open.

She went on again: 'I was just coming down, Amos.'

He said: 'I'll go on about my rounds.' He turned and passed through the door and closed it behind him.

The bed looked as if a battle had gone on atop it, he thought as he went back along the landing. 'I ought to beat that snake's haid in,' he said softly to himself. 'But I still owe him!'

He chuckled. Hell, he (Amos) had no bridle on Lily. But when a woman was his woman he liked her to stay that way until he figured there was an end to it. Seemed like this one had beaten him to the punch. Unless, of course, she figured she could have men on a string, two or three, maybe more. He didn't like that thought ... That Rainey, he surely was asking for it! But maybe Rainey, who looked part-Injun, was figuring, as in Injun might, that now he held Crowle's life he should have a share in that life too ...

But, hell, there were slews of women!

He went back to the office. Deputy Jake was still there.

'Make some coffee, Jake.'

'Sure, Amos.'

Crowle didn't tell Jake much. He never told anybody much. He was more likely to ask questions, and expect straight answers; and quick ones.

But it was Jake who, after patrolling later that day and as darkness was falling came in and volunteered some information, not without a certain note of triumph in his voice, too, as if silently adding 'I told you so'.

'That Rainey character's left town again—so Cal Lippton tells me.'

'Do tell,' said Crowle. For the second time in the last few days he wondered if he would ever see Rainey Jay Dodson again.

'You been out back lately, Amos?' asked Jake suddenly.

'No, I don't think so.'

'Looks like the privy got blown clean away, Amos.'

'The hole's still there ain't it?'

'Yes, the hole's still there.'

'What yuh worried about then, boy? Turn your ass to the sun an' to the moon.'

CHAPTER 6

It was deep night again when Dodson reached the hideout in the hills and, this time he made his presence known by a whistled signal to the lookout, who happened to be small redbearded Norte-Americano Fox Raymond.

'Rainey—anybody behind you?'

'No, do you think I'm that kind of jackass?'

'Guess not. Come ahead then.'

They reached the firelight, the men rising to their feet, and Jonquil saying, 'You have news for me, amigo?'

'You got some hot coffee there?'

'Sure.'

It was Felipe who handed over the steaming mug.

The men hunkered down again and,

reluctantly small Fox went back to his post.

'How did the storm catch you?' asked Dodson.

'We sheltered,' said Jonquil, noticeably impatient, the other boys seemed a mite edgy. 'A horse bolted, fell down the rocks, we had to shoot him. That was all.'

Dodson grimaced and spat a stream of brown liquid into the fire where it sizzled and black smoke rose. 'Phew-ee! Who made this?'

'I did,' said big Pat Grimson.

'It tastes like skunk-water.'

Taciturn Pat, not much of a one for repartee laughed loudly and immoderately and a few of the others followed suit.

'Bunch o' goddam jackasses,' bellowed Jonquil, thrusting a bottle of tequila at Dodson. 'Here, wash it down with that.'

Dodson held the bottle out to the firelight and saw that it was half-full.

He drew the cork out with his teeth and spat it into the fire. He took a deep swig. 'Coyote-piss,' he said. He cradled the bottle between his knees and grinned at the bandit-leader.

'You're an irritating bastard,' said Jonquil. 'What's the matter, you get thrown outa that town?'

Dodson's grin faded. 'The man isn't living who can throw me out of *any* town.'

'Oh, oh!' guffawed Jonquil. 'He bites.'

The two men measured each other across the fire and Dodson said, 'I came like I said I would. I always keep my promises. The town's in a mess. They're cleaning up. And they're also building a new schoolhouse roof on account of a dance they've got there on Saturday.'

'Which Saturday?'

'This Saturday.'

'Oh, oh!'

'Yeh. Oh, oh! There's been a killing there too. A little whore got herself cut up.'

'That'll keep the marshal busy.'

'Well, kinda.'

'Who'd kill a whore?'

'Me. I knew her from San Antonio and she knew I was wanted. I don't know what the reward is now but it ain't peanuts. It only needed a word to Amos Crowle. An' if he's got dodgers ...'

'You saved his life,' growled Harve Gould, speaking for the first time.

'Crowle's a lawman,' said Dodson. 'I walked right into that stupid little cow, right into her crib. I didn't know it was her until I was inside. Christ, she had come down in the world since I knew her before ...' Jonquil cut in: 'Does Crowle suspect anything do you think?'

'I did hear he suspected a little drummer who beat up on one of the girls in Mama Boola's cathouse in Mextown on that same night. The little bastard got himself killed in the storm though, out on the range.'

'Pity! Crowle might've been off chasing him.'

'I figure he hasn't forgotten Harve either,' said Dodson.

'An' I ain't forgot *him* neither,' growled Harve Gould.

Dodson, ignoring Harve, went on again: 'I jumped Crowle's woman.'

'You jumped ...'

'That Lily frail?' put in the persistent Harve.

'Yes.'

'Does Crowle know?' said Harve loudly, over Jonquil's laughter.

'I think so.'

'No wonder you left town.'

Now everybody was laughing: Felipe, Jonquil, Juan, Pat Grimson, Yank Brady. And Harve started up too. 'No wonder,' spluttering. 'An' she's a lovely filly, that gal. Sort of French. How was she, Rainey? Did she know any French tricks?'

'Plenty. But I know a few myself.'

'I've never met the senorita,' said Jonquil. 'You ain't just joshing us again are you, Rainey?'

'Nope. But I figured I best leave town before things got too complicated. I did'nt want to bring things to a head too soon. Besides, I'd planned to come tonight anyway, after the storm an' all. So mebbe Saturday, eh, Jonni?'

'Why not?'

Dodson finished the bottle of tequila and threw the bottle to crash on the rocks behind him. The laughter had died. 'I've been thinking,' he said and they all leaned forward a bit.

'One thing,' cut in Harve Gould presently.

'What's that?' said Jonni.

'Amos Crowle is mine.'

Jonni exchanged glances with Dodson, who nodded.

'All right,' said Jonni. 'Go on, Rainey.'

There had been no more rain for a day but the wind was still blustery. And, although this made for coolness and the people needed coolness it also caused difficulties while cleaning up of the town was under way, and particularly in the case of the schoolhouse roof. This job was under the supervision of hostler Cal Lippton who was a handyman par excellence. There was enough material to build a small fort, so Cal had no problems there. His problems were his labour-force, so many that they got in each others way, amateurish, untried. They got blown off the roof. They got knocked off the roof by their fellows. They tripped over their own feet or other folks' implements and fell off the roof. They banged themselves with hammers, sawed themselves with saws, cut themselves with cutting instruments and poked holes in themselves with pointed instruments.

It was a miracle that there were no actual broken limbs or heads. One younker got hit in the face by a swinging plank and finished up looking like a professional pugilist. But he was the only one who carried scars for more than a few days.

* * * *

It was a lovely evening. This time, strangely, there had not been any wind to speak of all day. The new improved log-and-clapboard schoolhouse roof looked almost too new and some folks said it ought to be painted or something. But there just had not been time.

Anyway, Cal Lippton, who was in charge of operations, had said that it ought to be left to get weathered first, and Cal seemed to know what he was talking about.

The town was almost back to normal after the storm; a real old-style Texas twister that had been!

Slashes of raw wood showed here and there, windows packed with box-ends while awaiting a glazier, a few doors still saggin on broken hinges. Most of the fences, if they had not been entirely blown away had been made to look neat again. A few privies were still minus doors and had been discreetly shielded by canvas or old curtains. Trudy Saunders, wife of the banker, had hung a fancy flowered drape in front of hers. The wind had torn it a bit at first, but now it only rippled exotically in the sunshine.

The jailhouse privy had been blown to hell and gone. On Friday night a drunk on his way home from Mextown fell in the hole and from stinking drunk became just stinking. No man got sober so fast!

When he was told about this incident, the marshal was in the Silver Horseman Saloon and he laughed fair to split his sides. Nobody in Logantown had seen him laugh before, only chuckle a few times.

A mighty unsettling sort of gent!

When he appeared at the dance on Saturday evening, though, he looked right smart. He looked like somebody who was somebody and nobody could deny that.

Things soon got under way. There was a four-man band consisting of a squeeze-box, two fiddles and a kettle-drum. Jack Trisket was caller for the dancing, having the biggest voice. Jack's missus, Addie, had been ailing of late, but she was there tonight and looked almost her old self, a plump and pretty woman.

Marshal Crowle took over the calling for a while so that Jack could dance sedately with Addie. The marshal did not seem to be dancing with anybody, though many a buxom female gave him a sidelong glance of invitation. Lily Duboissier was not there, and there were no girls, of course, from back o' town. They had their own business to attend to, one wag said, a different kind of dancing. The marshal and his deputy, Jake, had arranged between them to take spells at the dance, turn and turn about. When the scared Mexican boy ran through the door and among the dancers it was Crowle who was there and, alert as a mountain cat pounced on the youngster, making him more scared than ever. He learned from the trembling boy's garbled tale told in a mixture of Spanish and bastardised English that the boy had already been to the law office. A bunch of tough caballeros were tearing Mextown to pieces and one hombre had already been knifed to death. Deputy Jake had sent the boy on to the schoolhouse to notify the marshal and gone down to Mextown on his own.

'The goddam fool,' said Crowle.

Doc Lessiter was the nearest, heard everything, said: 'I'll get a gun and come with you, Amos.'

'No, Doc, thanks, but it's not your business to fight. You look after the boy, he shouldn't go back there yet. Will you?'

'Certainly, Amos.' Doc put his arm around the boy's thin shoulders. 'Come, amigo, we'll get you some sody-pop.'

But others were coming forward now:

Jack Trisket, undertaker Rab Gray, saloonkeeper Jerry Rand, storekeeper Bud Juleson, rancher Rollo Earle and some of his boys, Cal Lippton and his young assistant; even Mayor Blaine, shaking and burbling: they all wanted to help in any way they could.

They were threatening to get their guns, moving towards the doorway. The drink was in them. There was a plentiful supply of a fairly potent punch; and much of harder stuff too, circulating in bottles and hip-flasks.

Cookie-night, thought the marshal sardonically. He had never known such cooperation. He held up his hands.

'Hold it, gents. I don't think there's any need for a posse. This is probably just what you might call a storm in a tea-cup. You can't just go on the word of a frightened kid who ain't got much English. Jake's already gone to see what's happening. I'll join him. We'll see to things, me an' Jake, that's what you good folk are paying us for.'

Shit, he thought. But he could be nice and diplomatic if he had to be, even if it did make his belly crawl as if it were full of ants. And maybe he was misjudging these people.

Shy Jake Philpott's equally shy sweetheart, Arabella Juleson, ran forward. 'Will Jake be all right, Mr. Crowle?'

Her father, Bud, anticipated the marshal's reply. Putting his arm round his daughter's shoulders, he said, 'Sure Jake will be all right, honey. Young Jake ain't no forward-coming chatterbox but he certainly knows how to take care of himself.'

Crowle had collected his gun-rig and was on his way to the door.

He passed through it. Nobody followed him.

It was a balmy night, the town deserted, the stars pale. The marshal went cautiously at first, getting his eyes accustomed to the darkness after the brightness of the schoolhouse. All the townsfolk and their friends were at the dance.

This could have been a ghost town.

There was no sound from back at the schoolhouse, particularly now Crowle was getting further away. He did not think the band had started up again yet.

No doubt everybody was still chewing things over. He hoped nobody went off half-cocked. He began to run on his toes, keeping in the shadows. His broadcloth coat flapped open, facilitating easier access to his gun.

He heard Mextown some time before he reached it but it did not sound any different than usual. Of nights there was always a sort of frenetic buzz from down there. And shouts, laughter, screams, music, singing, a hodge-podge, a fluctuating cacaphonic all-over *buzz*. There were all sorts and conditions of folk there and, despite the name given to the place by worthies of Logantown proper—and Mextown was part of that after all, though some folks tried to pretend that it wasn't—all its inhabitants were not Mexes and *mestizos,* not by a long shot.

There was a narrow patch of rubbishy open land before the ill-defined beginnings of back o' town, as Amos Crowle preferred to call it. He paused on the edge and nothing moved. There were the usual window-lights on the other side.

He drew his gun before crossing the open space, half crouched, running now on the balls of his feet like an Indian. He wondered about Jake Philpott. Where was Jake? The Mexican boy had not given any specific information, and this place was a warren of dives and hovels.

He reached the other side of the open land without incident. Then a man came suddenly out of the shadows, hand uplifted. 'Marshal Crowle. Please, marshal.' The gink must have eyes like a cat, thought Crowle, saying harshly, 'You lookin' to get yourself shot?'

'There's been a killin', marshal. Over

here.' He wore a broad-brimmed sombrero and Crowle followed this.

Light gushed from a door suddenly flung wide and the Mexican led the marshal through into the interior of a cantina, sod-floored, with benches and a long table and the usual barrels and bottles and pails. People were clustered, and now the cluster parted to let the lawman through, until he came to a stop above the body which lay there, its blood dyeing red the hard black beaten-earth floor.

'Take the knife out of his throat for Christ's sake,' said Crowle.

A fat swarthy woman did this and stepped back quickly as more blood gushed in a small fountain from the torn jugular. In the background another woman was sobbing, a third murmuring soft comforting words in Spanish. The fat woman dropped the blood-dappled knife at Crowle's feet. It was a heavy blade, but thin, the point needle-sharp.

'The man threw, senor,' a male voice said. 'I have never seen a man throw a knife so well.'

Other voices confirmed this in a variety of dialects.

'What kind of man?'

'A young gringo. I have not seen heem before.'

Crowle bent quickly and picked up the bloodstained knife. He wiped it on his fine broadcloth pants where it left a shiny smear. He tucked it into his belt.

A redfaced American pushed his way forward. Crowle remembered having seen him around town: he was a regular barfly, and the rotgut was cheaper down here, particularly if you fancied tequila, pulque, mescal, or other more outlandish brews and concoctions.

'I've seen him before, marshal. The younker. You know him, marshal. I think he's a friend o' yourn.' The redfaced man leered. 'The feller who calls hisself by that fancy name, Rainey Jay.'

'You sure?'

'I'm sure.'

'He's right, marshal,' said another voice, coming from a little harmless, middleaged half-breed that Crowle also knew by sight. 'It was that young Dodson hellion all right. I've seed him in the Silver Horseman. He had other fellers with him an' one of 'em was Harve Gould. I didn't know any of the others.'

'I did,' said another voice. 'It was the one they call Jonquil.'

Crowle had heard of Jonquil. Who had not along the borderlands?

The tale was growing rapidly now as voices got bolder. It had been a fight over a girl that Dodson had wanted, who had belonged to the man on the floor. He had drawn a knife on Dodson, who had a knife too, and he threw faster and very straight.

The girl was pushed forward, bold-looking, bursting out of a low-cut blouse. Some of the voices became accusing. She liked teasing men, that one! She liked them to fight over her. José's blood was on her head. José staring sightlessly at the ceiling and taking no part in the recriminations.

Somebody said that the men—there had been half-a-dozen or more—had obviously been looking for trouble.

Crowle raised his gun in the air. 'My deputy?' he said. 'Where is my deputy?'

There was silence. He did not have to fire the gun. His voice had been loud and they had heard him.

'He went after them, marshal.'

Crowle was out in the night again when he heard the shooting, a sudden savage spattering of it which died as abruptly as it had begun.

Gun in hand, Crowle ran, half-crouching, keeping to the shadows.

Turning a corner, he tumbled over the prone figure of a man who made a throaty sound of agony as the boot bit into his side. Crowle went sprawling, losing his gun.

On hands and knees, he turned himself around and found himself face to face with his own deputy.

Jake raised his head, his face a drawn white mask.

'Almos! There's two of 'em out there. I think I got another one, though ... I'll be all right. Watch yourself ...'

'Jake ...' Crowle broke off, turning. A shape in the darkness; a voice saying softly, 'Marshal'. It was the Mexican with the big hat who had first led Crowle to the cantina. 'Can I help, marshal?'

'Yes, will you look after my friend?'

'I weell, marshal.'

Shots blasted from the darkness ahead. A bullet slammed into a log wall behind Crowle. Another took his hat off. The Mexican Samaritan had already taken cover. Crowle's gun was by his hand. He grabbed it and rolled. The serated butt was sticky with blood. Jake's blood.

The Mexican came out of hiding again, crouching. He had spunk. Jake was raising himself on one elbow. 'Get down, both of you,' Crowle snarled. Flattened against the log wall, one knee on the rock-hard ground, Crowle fanned the hammer of his gun.

The echoes died away and he did not know whether he had hit anything or not. He heard bootheels thudding. Not loudly, but plainly.

The sound was ahead of him.

He rose and began to run recklessly, though knowing that he only had one bullet left in his Colt and he had no spare with him either and would need to reload. This had been a night for dancing not for gunplay. Looking back, he saw the man with the big hat bending over Jake; then he lost sight of them in the darkness under the pale stars. He reached the edge of the same waste-ground he had crossed when he was on his way into Mextown. Ahead of him a man was running, lurching awkwardly from side to side in riding boots. Maybe the one who had been hit by Jake; maybe another. I wonder if I hit anything, thought Crowle sardonically. He raised his gun to the level of his shoulder, his arm stretched out in front of him and grasped the wrist of his gunhand tightly with his other hand, steadying it. He tried to draw a bead on the running man, which was a difficult thing to do. The jogging, lurching figure seemed to be dancing in front of his eyes in a sort of woolly mist.

But then the man stumbled and, in trying to regain his balance was held stiff, suspended, hands raised. And Crowle thumbed the hammer and felt the Colt buck in his fist, once only— but in the old familiar satisfying way. And the man arched backwards convulsively, came over, twisted, fell. Crowle waited, reloading his gun. Then he went forward and bent over the dead man. It was Harve Gould and his spine had been blown apart and he looked very surprised.

A gun boomed from the shadows of Logantown and Crowle heard the bullet go by, perilously close. As he ducked, stepping sideways at the same time he caught his foot in the sleeve of Harve's outstretched arm and the night spun around him and more gunfire blasted in his head. He glimpsed something coming up to meet him, something on this rubbish-littered ground, something that gleamed dully.

He could not save himself; his temple hit the gleaming object with a sickening bone-grinding impact and then he blacked-out completely.

After the shindig in the cantina the boys had split up. Two of them, Fox Raymond and Harve Gould stayed behind. Jonquil, Dodson, Yank Brady, Felipe, Juan and big Pat Grimson did a quick pasear round the backs of Logantown, making for their next objective.

Harve and Fox, staying behind in Mextown, had another job to do before they joined the rest of the gang. So far things had gone as planned, and sweetly. The boys had tasted their first blood, Rainey Jay Dodson had seen to that, the Mex hardcase going down, the knife sticking from his throat.

Then came the schoolhouse. And that went sweetly too.

And now Juan stood at the back of the schoolhouse and Felipe at the front. They paced back and forth so that they could see the sides of the building as well as the ends and glimpse each other from time to time and signal. Both front and back doors were now locked on the outside anyway. All the guns and belts had been taken from the racks inside the front door and, after adding to their armoury with selected items that took their fancy the boys had thrown the rest of the stuff out into the night.

Juan and Felipe had a shotgun each as well as the rest of their armoury. The folks inside had been told they had best keep away from doors and windows or the two Mexicans might just start blasting and men, women and kids might get badly hit. Although Juan and Felipe rubbed along quite well with the gringo members of the band, gringos were not exactly their favourite people. They would start shooting all right given half a chance. Jonquil had chosen his guards well. Besides—the rest of the gang had taken three hostages with them: the fat banker and his fancy wife and a little girl who belonged to another family, just happened to be the nearest at hand. Those folks in the schoolhouse knew what would happen to the hostages if anybody tried to put a crimp in things.

So Jonquil, Dodson, Yank and big Grimson were off with the hostages, first of all to visit the banker's house where he would pick up his keys; there was bound to be a certain amount of loot there too and the boys had come well-supplied with gunny-sacks.

The diversion in Mextown had been the start of it, and Harve Gould and Fox Raymond had been left there to take care of Crowle and his deputy. Harve and Fox had the element of surprise very well on their side and it should prove to be a fairly easy dry-gulch parlay. Amos Crowle had a formidable rep; but he was not immortal, had no magic armour against a hail of bullets from the dark.

After Harve and Fox had taken care of this murder-chore they were to have a quick look-in on Juan and Felipe to see if these two needed help, though that hardly seemed likely; but Jonquil was nothing but thorough. And after this Harve and Fox were to go down to the bank and, whether the rest had arrived there yet or not were to stay adjacent and keep their eyes peeled. Although most of the townfolk were at the dance, there would doubtless be one or two outcasts loafing around town.

The Jonquil Gang intended to fix this town good before they returned to the hills and anybody who got in their way would be eliminated without compunction.

They would *take* this town, strip it, rape it ...

CHAPTER 7

Fox Raymond came suddenly out of the darkness and Juan almost shot him.

'Do you always have to creep about like a goddam coyote, amigo?'

The little redbearded man danced like a monkey on a stick. 'Sorry. I wasn't sure ...'

'Where's Harve?'

'Harve's dead. Crowle got him. I got Crowle, though. An' we had fixed the deppity before that. Everythin' all right here?'

'Si. You have to go to the bank now.'

'I know.'

Juan watched Fox dissolve into the darkness; then he spat in the dust and continued his pacing. One man dead. Still, he had never really cottoned to

Harve Gould anyway.

He was glad about Crowle getting his, though. He had heard a lot about Crowle. That gringo had had a lot of devil in him. He had been the kind of caballero who was worth six Harves. Despite himself he suddenly felt a spasm of regret. On the other hand he hoped that Fox had made damned sure ...

Yank Brady stood outside the house. Jonquil, Dodson and Grimson had gone inside with the banker, his wife and the little girl. The kid had been quite amenable, still seemed to think this was some kind of game, all part of the shennanigans at the schoolhouse. The banker was a pompous old bastard. You could see that, deep down he was scared. His missus had spunk though. She was plump and pretty and just about the right age as far as Yank was concerned. He liked mature and experienced women; women with class and moxie. What was a woman like that doing with such a bag of wind for a husband?

Yank wished he was in the house with her right now. And, maybe while the others were looking for loot ...

Naw, Jonni would say when ...

Although Yank, of course, did not know it he had slightly misjudged Ephriam Saunders. In defence of the fat banker it must be said that, under the circumstances it would have been hard for any man to withstand the Jonquil gang's demands. For they used Ephriam's wife, Trudy and the little girl, whose name was Kath—she was the daughter of a small rancher who had numerous other offspring—as metaphorical clubs with which to beat Ephriam over the head. The stout man did not want to see his wife violated or tortured before his eyes or the little girl subjected to unmentionable things. He handed over his keys, and the bandit leader and the lean dark man called Dodson left Ephriam and the others guarded by the big untalkative hardcase and went off to ransack the house.

'Scum!' said Trudy.

The big man just looked at her and gave a little jerk of his gun as if to tell her to shut up.

The three captives sat on an ornate chaise-longue that Trudy had had brought by waggon from Houston.

Ephriam contemplated jumping the big man who was obviously not nearly so quick and vicious as the other two— or as the cold-eyed snake who had been left on guard outside.

But Ephriam knew in his heart that the big man was not *that* slow, was not *that* stupid and that all he, Ephriam would get for his bravado was a bullet in the head.

The little girl, Kath was twisting the hem of her dress around and around in her fingers and watching the big man with bright inquisitive eyes.

Then, suddenly Trudy said, 'Ep, I'm sorry, I feel faint. The way we were bundled along by this scum ...' She broke off with a little sigh, her head dropping onto her breast.

'My wife's sick,' said Ephriam and, looking up at the big man he began to rise.

'Stay where you are, uncle.'

Under the menace of the gun, Ephriam subsided once more. 'But my wife ...'

'I just want some water,' said Trudy weakly. 'Or maybe just a spot of brandy.'

'There's some brandy over there,' said Ephriam, pointing. 'Over on that little table by the wall.'

'Let the lady get it then.'

'All right, I can do that for myself,' said Trudy. 'Get out of my way.'

The big man grinned and stood to one side, his gun uplifted.

Swaying, watched anxiously by her husband, Trudy went past the man and over to the liquor table.

'Do you want one, Ep?' she asked,

half-turning.

Their guard was half-turned too, trying to watch the two on the chaise-longue and the woman by the table all at the same time.

'I'll have a small one, please,' said Ephriam.

The big man was grinning. Maybe he thought Trudy should offer him a drink too. But she pointedly did not.

As she began to return, balancing a balloon-shaped brandy glass with its contents in each hand, the big man, still grinning turned to watch her. Her hands came up and she flung the contents of both the glasses into his eyes. He dropped his gun and staggered backwards, clawing at his face.

Ephriam was so surprised that he was held for a moment. But his wife was not. She followed through all the way, lifting her daintily-shod foot and kicking the big man viciously in his genitals with the pointed toe of her dancing shoe.

The big fellow yelped and doubled over, his hands dropping from his streaming face to his crotch. The room was full of the sharp cloying odour of fine brandy. Trudy turned and grabbed the heavy tubby cut-glass brandy container. She had re-stoppered it; she gripped it by the neck and, as the big man bent forward she brought it down on the back of his head, knocking his hat off, smashing through, the glass splitting with a sound like a distant pistol-shot.

The stricken man gave a huge sigh and dropped to his knees, then forward disjointedly on his face. Bright blood welled through his thin muddy-coloured hair. Trudy stood looking down at him, her face dead-white, her eyes enormous.

She had already dropped the cracked decanter. And now panic seemed to suddenly overwhelm her. She gave a high, stricken yelp and turned and ran to the front door, flung it open, ran out onto the verandah.

'Trudy,' cried Ephriam, rising, lumbering forward.

'Hold it—or I'll put a bullet in your spine.'

It was the other two men: he had not heard them approach.

Ephriam halted. He turned slowly. The little girl Kath still sat in her place on the chaise-longue. She looked down at the prone form of Pat Grimson and began to giggle. The two hardcases, with their guns and their gunny-sacks came round and looked down at Grimson too and Jonquil swore fluently and obscenely in Spanish.

Look-out Yank Brady had much quicker reflexes than had his big pard, Pat Grimson who, although Yank didn't yet know it, now lay unconscious in the house. When the woman ran into him, Yank could hardly believe his luck. He had been wanting to get his hands on this one.

* * * *

Amos Crowle was fighting his way out of a barrel of molasses.

He was suffocating in this thick, nauseating darkness. The molasses tasted salty, strange. He thought he was drowning in this nauseating, cloying saltiness. He felt panic. He closed his mouth tightly and he whispered savage obscenities only in his mind.

But the mess *was* clearing slowly.

He was sitting up—and then the sky fell on his head, knocking him down again.

He tried it again. And this time he made it.

He stood swaying, looking about him and remembering. The shooting! But he did not think he had been hit. He had tripped over his own feet or something like a gawky schoolgirl and had fallen and hit his head.

Then he saw the body of Harve Gould again. Harve had been to blame, rot him! Something gleamed, half-buried in the ground. Part of a plough-share maybe. He could see his own blood gleaming on the sharp edges. There was a gash in his temple just beneath the hairline; it stung like hell. But his headache was getting better.

He saw his gun lying nearby and he picked it up and wiped it and put it back in its holster. Tucked into his belt he still had the throwing knife that had been taken from the throat of the dead Mexican back in the cantina.

There was no sound from the darkness around him, no movement. Maybe that drygulching bastard thinks he's finished me for keeps, thought Crowle savagely. He began to detect distant sounds of revelry from back in Mextown. A corpse now and then, here and there did not make much difference to those people. You only had one life. And corpses couldn't join in on anything, that was for sure.

He found his hat and put it on.

The schoolhouse, he thought.

He began to put one foot purposefully before the other.

* * * *

Jonquil pulled Yank Brady off the screaming woman and sent him sprawling.

Jonquil shook Trudy and, with a last final terrified gasp she shut up.

'Let's have no more of that, chiquita,' said Jonquil. 'He ain't hurt you. Not yet!'

Ephriam Saunders was trying to get at Yank, but Rainey Dodson's Colt jabbed into his soft belly stopped him dead.

The little girl, Kath ran to Trudy who, whimpering and with shaking fingers was trying to make herself look halfway decent again. Convulsively, the woman bent and picked up the child and held her tightly.

Pat Grimson stood in the background wiping his bleeding head with a huge bandanna.

'The bank,' said Jonquil. 'C'mon—move!'

Fox Raymond was waiting impatiently in the shadows. He told them about Harve, and Jonquil muttered a few expletives in Spanish.

'Good riddance,' said Dodson laconically.

Ephriam Saunders opened the bank and they all filed in except Fox and Grimson who stood on watch outside.

'What happened to you?' Fox wanted to know.

'I'm all right,' said Grimson, dully. A man passed on the other side of the street, singing softly to himself. He did not see the two figures in the shadows. It was quiet here. The breeze could be heard soughing gently out on the range. There were no lights.

Crowle waited until the Mexican had turned his back again and was holding the shotgun loosely.

And then Crowle moved out of the darkness, the knife in his hand.

Felipe had been an outlaw since he was a boy. He was a fast, alert man. He heard something, or sensed something; and he spun on his toes, lifting the shotgun again. Half-crouching, Crowle threw the knife with an under-arm sweep. The thin blade went in deeply beneath Felipe's breastbone and he groaned protestingly, dropping the shotgun which, fortunately did not go off and grabbing convulsively at the handle protruding from his body. But then the life went from him and with hardly a sound he flopped on his face on top of the shotgun.

Crowle rolled the body over with his foot and extracted the knife and wiped it on the dead man's buckskin vest. He took the shotgun and a Bowie knife the man had in the back of his belt. The hand-gun too.

He had already figured that there was most probably a guard at the back of the schoohouse too. He moved along the log wall, ducking low as he passed the lighted window. He reached the corner and looked around it to where the other man paced: another Mex with a shotgun. He waited a bit. Then, when Juan went to the corner to look for Felipe, Crowle cold-cocked him with the butt of a gun. Juan did not make a sound as Crowle caught him and lowered him gently to the ground.

Crowle stood motionless in the shadows for a few moments. Nothing moved. He took the second shotgun. He carried both shotguns to the back door and leaned one of them against the wall beside it.

With his free hand, he tried the door. It was locked but the large key was still in place. He turned the key and pushed the door, the shotgun in the crook of his other arm.

Out of the light Jack Trisket came at him with a broken chair-leg.

Jack stopped the powerful downward

132

swing just in time but still managed to give the marshal a nasty crack on his uplifted arm. The muzzle of the shotgun was about an inch from Trisket's swelling belly and the marshal's finger was crooked round the trigger.

The colour drained from Trisket's face and his eyes looked sick.

'I almost perforated you, Jack.'

'I didn't know it was you, Amos.'

Crowle grinned like a timber wolfe. 'I guess you owed me that one, Jack.'

'Sorry, Amos.'

The gang stripped the bank of bills, coin, gold-dust, valuables. Ephriam Saunders led the way. Behind him, Jonquil and Dodson filled gunny-sacks as they went along. Yank Brady had been left behind in the front office of the bank with Trudy Saunders and the little girl, Kath.

Ephriam could not bear to think of his wife being left again with that animal and, in his haste to get back to Trudy

133

he kept stumbling, fumbling, dropping his keys, forgetting his numbers while Rainey Dodson constantly goaded him with soft obscenities.

At last they were finished and, feeling as if his legs would hardly support him any longer, Ephriam staggered back to the front of the bank, the two robbers at his heels.

Trudy was sitting on a hard chair next to the counter with the child on her lap. The child was asleep. Trudy was not weeping now, just staring into space. Yank was leaning on the other end of the counter staring sullenly at the couple. None of the three people seemed to have moved a fraction since they were left there by Saunders, Jonquil and Dodson.

Jonquil said, 'There are surely other places we can strip.' He was not only thorough, he was greedy.

Dodson said, 'Stores, saloons, hotels ...'

'I mean to take this town,' said Jonquil, probably for the third or fourth time.

Dodson did not agree with him on this. But he said: 'I don't figure we need hostages anymore. Anyway,' he jerked a thumb, *'they've* outlived their usefulness.'

He had his gun out. Yank lifted his. 'One fat ol' hombre an' a woman an' a kid,' said Jonquil scornfully. 'They ain't gonna do us any harm. Lock 'em up someplace.'

They were finally shut into what was termed the bullion room, though now it was nothing more than a dusty storeroom full of harmless junk. It had a stout log door, however, and a shut-tered window with a padlock. Jonquil took all the bank's keys away with him and threw them out into the night. Fox was there, waiting, jittery as ever and, near him Grimson stood like a drugstore Indian. Nobody had bothered him.

They were in a hardware store and big

Pat Grimson had busted open the tin-can safe with a pick-axe and they were emptying it when Rainey Dodson said, 'I've got to go get my woman.'

He added: 'Plenty of pickings down there,' meaning around by Madam Lily's Cafe. It was by way of being the "commercial centre" of town.

'We won't be far away,' promised Jonquil.

CHAPTER 8

Everybody wanted to help the marshal, form a posse, a vigilante group, whatever you'd like to call it, go seeking the Jonquil gang, rid the town of them, the territory. And while Amos Crowle would not have dreamed of turning down all offers, he obviously had to turn down some.

He chose Jerry Rand of the Silver Horseman, rancher Rollo Earle, freightman Jack Trisket, liveryman Cal Lippton and storekeeper Bud Juleson.

Bud's daughter, Arrabella, who had been keeping company with the marshal's deputy, Jake Philpott, was almighty worried about him, her pretty face white, her eyes enormous. Crowle said Jake was hurt but would be all right. The marshal hoped he was speaking the truth. Jake was still in Mextown, most probably back in the cantina now with that big-hatted Mexican and his friends. Doc Lessiter said he figured he knew the place, he'd go down there Crowle told him not to pause on the way, not to take chances, those hellions were still on the prowl.

The gang had, of course, taken away all the weapons from the schoolhouse. But Crowle had two shotguns, two hand-guns and no less than three knives taken from the Mexican guards, as well as his own long-barreled Dragoon Colt and the knife he had brought back with him from Mextown, yanked from the throat of a dead man. The knife that had belonged to Rainey Jay Dodson. And now Crowle figured that maybe he didn't have to look any further than Dodson for the murder of the prostitute called Pearly Jane who had probably known something about that young hellion from way back.

So the posses weren't too badly off for armaments as they might have been. And, as they moved out Jack Trisket almost fell over another gun which had maybe been thrown away, but not far enough.

The front door of the schoolhouse was open behind them and some of the others stood there. Somebody had to stay with the womenfolk, somebody reliable. Crowle had picked Mayor Kit Blaine, storekeeper Thaddeus Rainbow and undertaker Rab Gray among others: non-combatants he considered them. The Mayor had expostulated. But you couldn't argue with the marshal for long, he just wasn't listening.

The area around the bank was deserted.

Crowle said: 'Jack—you and Jerry go round the back. Watch yourselves. If it's clear there, stay there, and don't move till I call you.'

'Right, Amos.'

Crowle waited till the two men had

disappeared into the shadows, then he led the other three to the large front door, which he was able to open. Crowle made a motion for his men to stay where they were and then he moved in alone. Nothing happened. His figure appeared again in the doorway so suddenly that Cal Lippton who was nearest started violently.

'Watch that,' hissed Crowle. 'C'mon —follow me.'

They were all inside the bank when they heard the child weeping: a distant thing like a sort of echo. While Rollo Earle went out back to get Jack Trisket and Jerry Rand, the others tried to locate the sources of the crying sound and finally did so. Matches were lit. Crowle tried the heavy door. It would not budge. There was no key. The child stopped crying and there was no sound then but the shuffling of feet as the three other men came in from the back.

'There's nothing out there,' said Jerry Rand.

'Mebbe they rode out,' said Cal Lipp-ton, scratching another match, the light fitful.

'We didn't hear no hosses,' said Jack Trisket.

'They could've led 'em until they got outside the town an' then mounted up.'

'Who's in there?'

'Mister an' Miz Saunders an' the kid, I guess.'

'Quiet,' snarled the marshal.

He rapped on the heavy door with the butt of his gun. 'Ephriam?'

There were scraping sounds from the other side of the door, then a male voice said, 'Who's that?'

'It's Marshal Crowle. Is there a key out here we can use?'

'It was in the door. They must have taken it away with them.'

'Are you all right?'

'It's stifling in here. The little girl's bad.'

'Will you get away from the door, Ephriam? I'm goin' to start shooting.'

There were more sounds. Then the banker called, 'Go ahead, Amos.'

Crowle levelled his gun at the locks and fired three shots so close together that they sounded like a rolling thunder-clap in the enclosed space, the darkness. Faces were fitfully lit by gunfire and then the glow died. There was the acrid tang of gunsmoke. Crowle pressed the ball of his foot against the door and it swung open.

* * * *

'I can't go away with you, Rainey,' said Lily Duboissier. 'My life's in this town now.'

Dodson said: 'You've got to forget this town, leave this town behind you. We're two of a kind, you and me, Lily. We could have a good life together, new places, new faces, money to burn, no sweating in goddam restaurants.'

'I've done enough running away.'

'Running away? Horse-shit! You've

got to keep moving, honey. Like me. You're one of that kind ...'

'I can't, Rainey.'

'You're not still sweet on Amos Crowle? You can forget him.'

'What do you mean? What's happened to Amos? What's going on, Rainey? Something's going on isn't it? I thought you had left town. What did you come back for, Rainey?'

'I came back for you. I want to take you away with me. I want to share my life with you.'

'What kind of a life, Rainey? Killing, robbing, running from the law? We're not two of a kind, Rainey. But I know your kind. You'd either get me shot or drop me as soon as you got tired of me.'

'You didn't talk like that the other day.'

'That was a different thing.'

'Was it? As soon as we first saw each other we knew it was going to happen, though, didn't we?'

'That doesn't mean that I have to

follow you, leave my own life behind just because you say so. You come, you go. What did you really come back for, Rainey, and what has Amos Crowle to do with it?'

'I didn't say Crowle had anything to do with it. Except he was your man.'

'Perhaps he still is.'

'Not Amos.' Then another thought seemed to strike Dodson and he began to chuckle.

But then he heard the three shots and he stiffened visibly.

'What's happening in this town?' Lily cried.

Rainey went over to the window. Three shots! Not shotgun blasts, so they could not have come from Juan or Felipe. Nor could it have been Jonquil signalling those two to join the rest.

Lily joined him at the window. There were a few lighted windows out there. Not many. There was silence again.

'What's going on?' said Lily.

They both whirled as the door opened

behind them. Dodson went for his gun.

'Hold it, keed,' said Jonquil.

He was bareheaded, his sombrero hanging on his back by its chin-string, the white slash in his black hair gleaming under the lamplight. 'You're taking too long, Rainey.' His dark face lit up with a half-grin, half-leer.

'There's somethin' happening. Didn't you hear the shots?' He did not wait for an answer. 'Mebbe somebody's busted out of the schoolhouse. We've got enough. C'mon, let's get going. Bring the leetle lady with you if you want to. We might need another hostage now. She might come in mighty useful.'

'I'll kill the first man who touches her,' said Dodson levelly.

Jonquil laughed. 'I guess you would at that.'

Lily had been looking from one to the other of them, back and forth, her eyes wide. Now she started for the door but Jonquil, who had stepped away from it stepped back again, barring her way. She turned towards Dodson and her mouth opened in a silent cry. He had his gun levelled at her. 'You're coming with me, Lily. I want you. The hard way or the easy way, it's up to you.'

'Rainey!'

'Move!'

'Come on, lady, an' quietly,' said Jonquil. 'I wouldn't like to hafta put a gag between your purty leetle teeth.'

* * * *

Trudy and Ephriam Saunders and the little girl Kath had been sent back to the schoolhouse and the posse was advancing down main street.

Crowle, Trisket and Rand took one sidewalk. Juleson, Lippton and Earle took the other. Maybe the raiders had already left town and they would have to go out after them and valuable time was now being wasted. But they could not be sure. They would look pretty

146

damn' silly if they rode out and left the town at the mercy of those hellions while the posse chased the wind.

An aged man who kept a little harness shop ran onto the sidewalk and clutched the marshal's arm. The bandits had been there and taken his money. Oh, five minutes ago maybe! There was no sign of them now.

On the other side of the street Rollo Earle ran into a little *puta* who often prowled in this area. A lobo-faced gringo with a filthy mouth had tried to rape her but had not succeeded. She had a nasty bruise on her face and he had the mark of her nails on his. She liked to pick her men, and not pizen-scum like that one. If one of the man's amigos had not interrupted, said there was no time, that coyote might have killed her.

There was silence in that part of town again, except for the sibilent scraping sounds of the stealthy bootheels of the posse on the boardwalks.

They had to keep hard rein on their

jumpy nerves. It would be a terrible thing if one of them blasted a fellow-townsman by mistake.

And this, had they but known it, might well have been the case for in the particular paths they took they were not likely to run into any of the gang—they, at that time, were moving in the other direction and along the back of town, behind the buildings.

Marshal Crowle might have anticipated this and split his force. But they were not professionals, and he had figured he ought to keep them all in sight as much as possible, particularly as they were after a bunch of long-term owlhooters and killers like the Jonquil mob ...

So, like ships passing in the night on a dark and fog-ridden sea the Jonquil boys and the Logantown posse went their separate ways. And so it would be for some time ...

Yank Brady, who already bore Mexican wildcat scratches on his white

Yankee jib fell into the unguarded privy-hole behind the gaol and came up smelling like the skunk he was.

Jonquil, almost exploding with suppressed mirth sent Yank ahead to ready the horses. 'We can foller you by the stink,' he spluttered.

'How about the hosses then?' Fox Raymond wanted to know. If they get upwind o' that they're liable to panic.'

'We'll have to take that chance,' said Jonquil. 'I don't think I'm goin' to risk firing signal-shots for Felipe and Juan. Fox, you creep around there an' tell 'em. It ain't far out of your way.'

It looked for a moment as if Fox was going to give Jonquil an argument. 'Go on,' said the leader. He was not even smiling now and his voice was mean. Fox went without a word.

Rainey Dodson led the girl, she silent now, stumbling along. She seemed kind of stupefied.

Yank was waiting with the restive horses in a grove of trees on the edge of town. Dodson had stolen another horse and a saddle for the girl and this Yank had already taken on ahead. This one was even more restive than the others and Yank was having a job to hold him.

Fox came back. He was breathless. 'I only saw Felipe. Lying out front o' the schoolhouse. He'd been knifed. Dead as stinkin' mackerel. No sign of Juan at all.'

As they were moving out, the girl began to yell for help.

Jonquil drew his gun. 'Shut her up, amigo, or I'll kill her now.'

Dodson reached out and hit Lily across the face with his hand, rocking her in the saddle. 'He means what he says, honey.'

She shut up, held on. She was not dressed for riding, mounted astride, her skirts hiked up, her silk-clad knees revealed.

Back in town the posse heard the thin cries, the thud of hooves.

'God, they've got a woman with them,' said Bud Juleson.

Amos Crowle turned about. They all hurried for the stables.

'I reckon we've got a good start anyway,' said Jonquil.

'I dunno,' said Dodson. 'If we want to protect your favourite hideout, Jonni, it might be best to go right through the hills and across the river into Mexico.'

'It's a long ride, Rainey.'

Jonni lapsed into silence, as if thinking. But he suddenly burst out distractedly. 'Would you mind ridin' the other side o' me, Yank?'

Brady muttered a few obscenities and nudged his horse in a half-circle.

'I've got a better idea.' Jonni was talking turkey again. *We'll go to Priest's Town.*

'These hills,' said rancher Rollo Earle. 'They're like damned honeycomb. I lost some mavericks in there once an' me an' two o' my boys almost got lost too lookin' for 'em. We never did find them little critturs. Mebbe they was rustled. Mebbe that Mexican coyote an' his boys ate 'em.'

They were in the foothills when Bud Juleson's horse stumbled and came down heavily. Its leg was broken. Though they were hard men, they were men who had a special love of horses and they had to risk a shot and put the beast out of its agony. Bud got up behind Rollo and eventually they began to lag behind. But then, after a while all of them had to dismount and lead their beasts and the terrain became perilous. Juleson and Earle became rearguard. Nobody poured lead at anybody. It was a good night, with a moon, pinpricks of stars, a small wind.

There was silence except for the clatter of hooves and bootheels, an occasional snort, a curse, a panted breath.

When they halted the silence seemed

absolute except for the warm and sighing wind.

After a while, Rollo Earle, who knew the territory better than any of them came up front and led the way.

They broke through the hills and the waters of the Rio Grande gleamed below them.

'Mexico's outa my jurisdiction,' said Marshal Crowle. 'Anyway, I reckon you boys have had enough. We'll go back to town ...'

'For now,' he added darkly.

Nobody argued with him. When he turned his horse and set off back the way they had come they all followed dociley behind him.

CHAPTER 9

Deputy Jake Philpott had a nasty wound in his side and would have to rest up for a while. But nothing vital had been touched, said Doc Lessiter; and Jake's sweetheart, Arabella was already in attendance ministering to her wounded hero like a sweet angel. But other folks had not been as lucky as Jake and now it was burying-time in Logantown.

The bodies of Harve Gould and his Mexican compadre, Felipe were soon shuffled into the ground. Then it was the turn of the little whore, Pearly Jane and another Mexican, the small-town Lothario (real name Esteban) who had been knifed by Rainey Jay Dodson.

Lastly but not leastly it seemed it was the turn of the little drummer—name,

Grimmons—who after leaving town with his horse and gig had been caught by the storm out on the range. His horse bolted, his gig had overturned, he had been thrown violently against a rock, his head stove in. He had sold finery to the local cathouse queen, Mama Boola, who was very fat and had dyed black hair and a moustache to match. He had also been a "friend" to many of Mama Boola's girls. He was a man it seemed who liked to beat up on his woman and more than one of the girls bore cuts and bruises that were mementoes of his last visit. It was thought that Grimmons had left town on the night that freelance whore Pearly Jane, who was detested by Mama Boola, had died. Or maybe he had left on the following day anyway. It was rumoured that Marshal Crowle had suspected Grimmons of being Pearly Jane's killer ... But now everybody was giving the little dead cuss the benefit of the doubt, including Mama Boola, who arranged for his funeral. In many ways, Mama was a very tolerant lady. Or maybe it was that this gesture was yet another way of cocking a snoot, exemplified by marching, wailing whores, at the goodwives of Logantown.

The Mexican bandit, Juan, now languishing in jail with a bandaged head wanted to know from Doc Lessiter what had happened to his good amigo, Felipe. Doc told him of Marshal Crowle and the knife from the darkness and Juan's soulful eyes widened and he shrugged his shoulders fatalistically.

'That Black Heart man,' he said, 'he was supposed to be dead. He ess a devil.'

He ain't no angel an' that's a fact,' said Doc. 'Dead he could of been, but somebody couldn't shoot straight and now, like you, all he has is a sore head.

Juan continued to be in superstitious dread of Crowle who now had little difficulty in getting info from him as to the makeup of Jonquil gang and the approximate setting of their hideout on this side of the border. Crowle figured that they mightn't be in that hideout now anyway, but he decided he'd like to take a looksee just in case. And no posse hanging on his shirttails this time either!

It had been broiling hot in the valley lands of the Rio Bravo and, with twilight the gang was glad to rest. Jonquil wouldn't leave them in peace for long, however, saying it was better to continue in the cool of the night. He had a destination in mind. They had long since passed the old hideout: that would be left for the indolent times, the waiting times. Jonni knew that Amos Crowle, a seasoned manhunter might also be willing to play the waiting game. But Crowle was a crafty cat too, and you could never be quite sure which way a cat might jump. Even so, the gang were tired of being pushed, and the chief complainers were Yank Brady and, of course, Dodson's woman, Lily Duboissier. And there was something between Yank and the woman, far more than there was between Lily and any of the rest who tolerated her because she was Rainey's property.

It was obvious that Yank both wanted her and hated her; hated her partly because she *was* Rainey's woman and partly because she was beautiful and the perverted white-faced Eastern-city slug turned Western bandido just naturally hated anything beautiful and wanted to destroy it.

Yank had already suggested, and more than once, that the girl be left on the trail, after they had all taken turns at her first of course. The first time, Rainey Jay Dodson had ignored this suggestion. The second time he had said:

'Mebbe you'd like to go through me first, Yank, you an' that big gun o' yourn.'

Jonni said if he heard any more gab-gab of this sort he would personally take a hand. But, when Lily's grumblings became even more vocal and shrill the bandit leader growled, 'Just remember what your friend, Yank has proposed, lady.'

And this time Rainey hadn't said a word. And Lily had realised that her man, if he was that didn't really intend to precipitate anything yet awhile, woman or no woman.

The little bunch were all riding in lethargic taciturnity when big Pat Grimson suddenly fell off his horse.

Everybody else dismounted. They clustered around the large bulk on the ground. Grimson lay motionless on his back, his hat fallen off, his eyes closed, the big face white under the pale stars. Everybody bent forward, and Rainey Jay Dodson got down on one knee and lifted Grimson's head. When he took his hand away again his riding glove was sticky with blood. He said:

'The knock that shrill filly gave him back in town must have done more damage than we thought. Somep'n's busted open here.'

The horses were restless, not held now. 'Watch them critturs, Yank,' said Jonquil and the lean vulpine-faced man backed away from the circle. Grimson began to moan. 'He's comin' round,' said Jonquil. 'Maybe I could do something,' said Lily.

They were a tight circle.

'All right,' said Yank Brady's harsh voice. 'Turn round slowly, all of you, an' stick your hands in the air. A jerky movement from any one o' you an' I start blasting.'

For a split moment the five people froze like statues, then they slowly turned, their hands going over their heads in a cluster. Brady had a shotgun on them and it was rock-steady and they were in a tight knot in direct line with the wicked twin muzzles.

Fox Raymond said: 'That's my shotgun.'

Brady said: 'I borrowed it, Fox.'

160

Jonquil said: *'Hijo de puta!'*

Brady said: 'And you, Jonni.' He had been around low-born Mexicans and *mestizos* for quite a while now and was familiar with their deadlier insults. Having the whiphand now, Yank could afford to ignore such childishness. 'You lady, c'mon over here. Move!'

Hesitantly, Lily moved forward. And Brady went on: 'You take them gunny-sacks off Jonni's an' Rainey's hosses an' you put 'em on mine. You fix 'em tight now or it'll be the worse for you I promise that. And, gents, while the little lady's doing that you unbuckle your gunbelts with your left hands and you let them drop.'

The peril of the twin shotgun-muzzles was too great to be overlooked: nobody among the tired men felt like taking a chance. They let their gunbelts fall and, on Brady's further instructions kicked the gear nearer to him. Soon Lily had done her job with the gunny-sacks and Brady told her to gather up the gun-gear and, keeping out of the line of fire move back with him. She staggered a little under the load. Then, following Brady's instructions once more she threw the hardware as far as she could, almost precipitating herself on her face as she did so.

Brady then made the girl get on her horse. He climbed into his own saddle. He was an agile man. He didn't give the others a chance to make a dive for him. Nobody wanted a shotgun blast in the face. 'You better shoot us all right now, Yank,' said Jonquil. 'Cos, if you don't we'll get you later.'

Yank knew he just couldn't get them all: one of them would be bound to get him. He grinned and said: 'You take them reins now, honey, an' when I give the word you move that hoss fast. An' don't you fall off or I swear I'll ride over you.'

Lily Duboissier managed to do as she had been told. She did not fall off the horse. 'Let's go!' yelled Brady. There was dust and frenzied horses and the clatter of hooves, the sound becoming quickly less, the night swallowing the runaways. 'He took my goddam shotgun,' said Fox Raymond petulantly.

'He took everythin',' said Jonquil in high-pitched incredulity. 'Everythin'!'

They found the gun-gear pretty quickly but it took them almost an hour to catch all the horses. The last one turned out to be Pat Grimson's mount and he had gone in a circle and returned to his master's body, was standing over the prone form, his head hanging, his reins dangling. He was blowing, pegged-out. Dodson got down on one knee. 'Pat's dead,' he said.

'Let's go,' said Jonquil impatiently.

Dodson began to chuckle softly, humourlessly. 'His gun was right here in his belt. None of us thought to make a put for it even when Yank was still in range.' He yanked Grimson's gunbelt, complete with its forty-five from around the thick waist and tossed it over the saddle of the big man's mount. 'So now we've got a spare nag.'

'Let's go,' said Jonquil again.

There was no more talk about pushing for the place Jonni had called Priest's Town. They went back the way they had come, the riderless horse trotting beside Dodson and his mount. They didn't worry about a posse anymore, just about getting Yank Brady and the haul he carried. 'Do you think he'll go back to the hideout?' said Fox Raymond.

'What, an' wait to pick us all off or somethin'?' scoffed Dodson.

Jonquil said: 'I think he'll push on right through. He's got one hell of a start.'

'He'll go round the town that's for sure,' said Dodson. 'An' he'll have daylight on his side by then I guess. He'll push all right. He'll push.'

None of them mentioned the girl.

It was early morning and Marshal Crowle had his horse outside the law-office and was ready to go. His deputy sat in a big wooden armchair on the stoop with a shotgun across his knees. He had his arm in a sling and looked a bit whiter than usual but he was upright enough and his eyes were bright. He said:

'Don't worry about me, Amos. I'll look after things here. You watch your ass out there. That bunch of hellions might have come back to their hideout.'

Crowle said: 'I'll take care. It's just that I gotta do somep'n. Mebbe I'll learn somep'n from the hideout, if I find it. If that Mex back there,' he jerked a thumb, 'has given me a wrong steer I'll come back an' beat his teeth in.'

'I don't think he has. He thinks you're kinda supernatural or something, Amos.'

'Yeh.'

'Do you want us to come out lookin', if you don't come back within a certain time that is?'

'I'll be back.'

'All right, Amos.'

Crowle climbed into the saddle and, with a wave of his hand rode off. Arabella Juleson came out of her father's stores down the street and, as he passed her the marshal doffed his hat. Arabella gave a little bob of her head and Jake saw her smile. She walked towards the law-office and as she got nearer she smiled for Crowle's deputy too, and also gave him a mocking pseudo-military salute. He saluted back, waiting, watching. He liked the way that girl moved. He liked everything about her. He decided it was time he asked her to marry him, if he could get his halting tongue around the right words.

Amos Crowle set his horse at a steady mile-eating jog-trot. His, and the horse's difficulties would start when he got to the hills, but he had a couple of full canteens of water and a bag of cold grub. He was well-armed too. He was not pushing or anything; he was easy. But he figured he was ready for any eventuality.

It was going to be another broiling day, despite the recent rain and the temporary cool. He saw the hills at last but by that time they were shimmering in a heat-haze. He hadn't seen a soul during his journey so far, no animal even, nothing. He reined in and took a short nip at one of his canteens and wet a spare bandanna and laved his horse's nose and mouth. Then they went on and he didn't push the beast too hard and pretty soon they were on rocky ground and beginning to climb.

He tried to keep in mind the directions that the Mexican jailbird, Juan had given him. There, for instance was the mesquite outcrop rising from the ground like a misshapen monster!

Passing this, he dismounted and ground-hitched the horse and went forward a little way on foot. The rocky terrain was becoming steeper and more perilous; but Juan had said that a horse could be taken up there if the right trail was found. The day was still and quiet, the heat appearing to deaden things. There was just the hum of insects, and, behind Crowle his horse made tiny chittering, jingling sounds. Then something else impinged on that man's hearing, his senses; he stiffened; and then he slowly got down on his knees and bent and placed his ear to the rock floor. The heat of it assailed him. He could hear the soft thud-thud of the approaching horses like the quickening of his own heart. They were a long way off yet. But they were coming in this direction!

They were on a narrow trail which fell away in a steep slope on the lefthand side when Crowle and his horse came round the bend and into their path, Crowle with his Colt levelled, his other hand loosely on the reins.

'Amos,' cried Lily Duboissier.

Maybe her nervous urgency was

communicated to the beast she bestrode. Maybe, as she cried out she involuntarily pressed her knees to the animal's flanks. Whatever the reason, he moved forward, away from the other horse that had been so close to his side. Yank Brady had been riding all along with the shotgun across the saddle in front of him, one hand on the weapon's stock while the other held the reins. The movement of Lily's horse, partially obscuring as it did Crowle's view of Brady gave the outlaw his chance and, like a striking snake he took it, elevating the muzzle of the shotgun and pressing the trigger, the charge blasting its way past his horse's neck.

Crowle's mount screamed shrilly as it took the shot. It reared and pitched sideways and Crowle fell onto the least perilous side of the trail. But the horse tumbled in the other direction and crashed down the slope, raising a cloud of dust. At the same time Lily's mount carried her past the spot where the shot horse and its rider had been, past Crowle upon the ground. Brady swung his shotgun, ready to let the second charge go but, by this time Crowle had come to rest the right way up and he still had his hand-gun clutched in his fist. Jack-knifed into a seated position, he let off three closely-spaced shots, one of which hit Brady in the side just above his hip, the other two getting him higher up, in the chest, their violence throwing him backwards. His fingers, contracting on the shotgun trigger blasted off the second charge, sending slugs whining away into space and awakening more echoes in the heated stillness.

Brady went backwards out of the saddle and over the horse's rump, his upflung arms throwing the shotgun away from him to clatter down the slope to where the dust was still drifting around the shattered carcase of Crowle's horse. Brady's own mount bolted along the perilous trail but came to a stop before Lily and her horse, which the girl now turned gingerly around to face Crowle.

He stood upright now, his smoking gun in his hand as he looked down at the motionless form of Brady. He moved to the edge of the trail and looked down the slope to where the dust was settling now on the body of the horse, Brady's shotgun near, winking as the sun's rays caught it.

As Lily watched, Crowle returned to the body of Yank Brady. Lily heard him say explosively, 'The stinkin' son of a bitch'. Then he booted the body and it rolled over the edge and down the slope, raising more dust now, coming to rest near the body of Crowle's horse and within an arm's length of the shotgun.

CHAPTER 10

The falling shale stopped pattering. The dust settled again. Lily Duboissier slid sideways from her saddle and fell in an untidy heap on the trail. When Crowle reached her she was still conscious, but her eyes flickered and her face was paper-white beneath its coating of dust. Her lips were almost as white as her face and they were cracked and, as she tried to lick them with her tongue a spasm of pain distorted her features. She was no longer beautiful, but like a doll mutilated and thrown away.

'Your horse, Amos,' she whispered, 'it was my fault.'

Crowle said nothing. He took off his scuffed and rumpled leather vest and rolled it and put it beneath her head.

The two horses—Lily's and Brady's—now stood patiently waiting. Trying the girl's horse first, Crowle discovered that the canteen on the saddle horn was dry. He went to the dead man's horse and ran his hands over the gunny-sacks that festooned it, muttering expletives under his breath the while. He didn't pause then to open any of the sacks but he found the canteen and inspected that, finding a modicum of liquid in it. He took the canteen to Lily and she clutched it eagerly but then began to shake so much that he had to help her raise it to her lips.

There wasn't much water. She took it all. He left her again, left the trail, skidded down the slope, digging his heels into the shale and the soil, raising the dust again. He took the canteens from his dead horse, discovering that neither of them had been damaged in the fall. One of them was completely full and the other half-full. He climbed back to Lily. Her eyes were closed and she breathed with a rasping sound. She had let the empty canteen fall to her side. Crowle gave her some more water and, although she didn't open her eyes she sucked greedily.

'Not too much,' he said. 'Not too much.'

He took the canteen away from her. Her eyes flickered open and she raised one hand to shield them from the sun.

She said: 'Amos. The gang. He robbed them. They'll be after us.'

'How many? Did he shoot any of 'em?'

'No. There—there was four of them.' Her voice was becoming weak, her eyes less bright. 'No, one of them was badly hurt. I think he was dying ...'

'Rest,' said Crowle. Only three men, he thought. Maybe. An ambush, he thought. *Maybe.* But then there was the girl, she wasn't looking good, he ought to get her back to Logantown and Doc Lessiter just as soon as he could.

He went back to the dead outlaw's

horse and he took a look inside one of the gunny-sacks, felt the others with probing fingers. There hadn't been an inventory yet back in Logantown, there hadn't been time for it. Unless it was being taken right now. However, it looked as if that dead thief had been running with most, if not all the boodle that the Jonquil gang had captured from the town.

Crowle made up his mind what to do and he went back to Lily.

Jonquil had changed his mind. And he said: 'Our canteens are empty an' we need water an' the nearest place to get it is at the hideout.'

Fox Raymond said: 'Yank an' the girl didn't have any water either.'

Jonquil said: 'If they stopped at the hideout to get water they'll have been and gone by now. I figure Yank will keep on running.'

Rainey Jay Dodson said: 'Yeh, I'm inclined to agree with you, Jonni. But still an' all that hideout's dandy bushwack area if Yank decided to use it that way.'

Jonquil said: 'All right then, amigos, we'll split up. Three ways. And we'll approach the hideout from three different directions.'

They did just this. And none of them took a shot at a compadre and they discovered that the hideout hadn't been disturbed since they themselves had left it. They replenished their canteens at the stream and watered the horses and had a quick splash in the clear, shallow water. But still they were weary, frustrated. Raising his hands above his head as he stretched his stiffening body Jonquil released a stream of obscene and bastardised Spanish into the still air. But then, hands still raised, one of them in pointed signal, he stiffed, saying in English, 'Buzzards. Look at 'em. Buzzards!'

They were wheeling in the sky and coming lower and some of them were already plummeting to the earth.

The three men mounted and rode, each of them now with his gun in his hand.

They looked down at the obscene black mess of ungainly birds squabbling noisily over the carrion. 'No shooting,' said Jonni, holstering his own weapon, his men following suit. Dismounting, they began to pick up rocks. They scrambled down the slopes, pelting the buzzards at the same time. The carrion birds complained shrilly as they rose, wheeled away, only to hover in space, watching, waiting. Fox Raymond, small, lightweight was the first to reach comparatively level terrain and he shouted over his shoulder, 'There's a man's body down here.'

They all drew their guns again, looking about them. Finally they were closer together and the dust began to settle and in the sky above the wheeling buzzards screamed abuse. The men were unprotected. But nothing happened.

They didn't reholster their guns, however. And Fox Raymond said: 'It's Yank.'

Jonquil said: 'And the hoss, of course, compadres. But there ees no sign of the girl.'

Rainey Dodson said: 'There's no sign of the gunny-sacks Yank took either. An' another thing—that ain't Yank's hoss.'

The three of them grouped themselves a little uncertainly around Yank's body. They had all obviously half-decided that if they had been set-up for a drygulch parlay it would have by now taken place and they too would have been buzzard-bait. But they still held onto their guns. The body of the late New York hard-hat was almost naked, the clothes having been torn away, with gobbets of flesh too. But when Dodson affirmed that Yank had been shot to death before the buzzards got at him, the other two men agreed.

'Three slugs,' said Rainey, 'two of

'em plumb in the chest an' close together. That's mighty purty shootin'.' With the two other men watching him Dodson ranged away from the body and finally came to a stop beside the mutilated horse. 'This nag was shot too. Looks like a shotgun blast. And I recognise the beast. It belonged to Amos Crowle.'

Jonquil said: 'So Crowle was sashaying around in the hills. Trying to pick up our trail I guess. And he ran into Yank and the girl.'

'Looks that way. Explains the fancy shooting too. Them slugs in Yank look like they came from a handgun used purty close.'

Fox Raymond said: 'An' Crowle took Yank's hoss an' the girl?'

'Looks that way,' said Dodson again.

Jonquil began to curse in Spanish again. Then he quit that and started to laugh loudly, throwing his head back and braying to the skies so that he startled the vultures that had been slowly, slyly dropping nearer and they rose again, flapping, ungainly, squawking their protests.

The horrendous birds weren't the only creatures to be startled. 'F'r Christ's sake, Jonni!' exploded Rainey Dodson. The Mexican leader's habit of roaring with laughter at the most inappropriate moments was beginning to irk the lean young gunslinger. After losing both his girl and his share of the boodle, Rainey wasn't as cool as he used to be. Jonni's mirth subsided a little. 'You've got to hand it to that Crowle,' he spluttered. 'You really have.'

Dodson said: 'It was luck. Good luck for him, bad luck for us.'

'Bad luck for Yank, too. Crowle certainly made good use of *hees* luck.'

'Pity.' Dodson made a negligent poke of his boot towards the tattered corpse. 'I wanted to get this bastard myself.'

'An' Crowle took your girl,' mocked Jonquil.

'She was his girl first an' he's

welcome to her back. It's the haul that counts the most.'

'Rainey, amigo, you're a *charro* after my own heart. So we get the haul back, huh?'

'It ain't gonna be so easy this time. If we ride right into that town Crowle will be waiting for us. An' he's got friends.'

'But we've got friends also, amigo. Huh, *huh?*' Jonquil began to laugh again as the three men climbed back up the slope and the vultures wheeled lower once more, their cries becoming plaintive. They would start to scream and squabble again, however, when they reached the ground and the delicacies that awaited them there.

Lily Duboissier was back at her place and in the capable hands of Doc Lessiter. And now the centre of interest in town was the marshal's office where Crowle had the gunny-sacks opened. Their contents were brought forth and the folks gathered to watch, to point and exclaim, the senior folk, who had all managed to crowd in picking up items from time to time. Although the Jonquil boys had picked at the town like vultures seeking titbits, the bulk of the haul had of course come from the bank and from Trudy and Ephriam Saunders' home. The fat banker produced an inventory and began to tick things off as they came to light from the sacks. Money, valuables. Even a few papers that would have been no use to the bandits, that they had obviously grabbed in a hurry.

Amos Crowle said: 'Evidently they didn't stop to divvy up.' He had figured from some things that Lily had said that the gang had planned to light down at some settlement on the border before working things out. Priest's Town she had called it. He didn't know it.

None of the townsfolk seemed to know of it either, didn't seem interested. 'That's mine,' they said. *'That's mine!'*

They seemed as if they wanted to collect and hold things for a while before handing them once more (if ever) to Banker Saunders' safe-keeping. The fat banker, sweating profusely, ticked names off on his list and made notes in a cardboard-covered ledger.

It was almost as if Marshal Crowle was reading the fat man's mind. For the marshal now said: 'I think that's a good idee of yourn, Ephriam, you've had enough on your plate lately, an' that's a fact.' He laughed, a harsh sardonic sound. 'I don't reckon that folks want their money back as well though, do they?'

There was a chorus of 'No. No. Oh, no' and not a few sheepish looks to go with it.

It was evident that the surviving members of the Jonquil Gang had not followed Lily Duboissier and the marshal to the portals of Logantown. And Crowle, for one hadn't imagined that they would, had figured that Jonquil

183

and Dodson at least were too professional to take fool chances. But Crowle himself was also too professional to try and fool himself into thinking that Jonquil and Co. would lie doggo forever.

According to Lily there were only three men left. But Crowle didn't delude himself into thinking that Jonquil couldn't get more if he chose. The borderlands were full of scum who would kill for a handful of pesos. Crowle decided to wait awhile, here in Logantown. He figured Jonquil would *need* more men.

Although he couldn't be sure of this, of course, he (Crowle) was right in his assumption. If he could have followed the three owlhooters home ...

Temporary home anyway ... And *not* Priest's Town.

They sat in the huge high-ceiling sitting-room of a hacienda, close together, the three of them at the end of a long mahogany table with outsized intricately-carved legs. On the table-top in front of them were two bottles of tequila, one of them almost empty, three glasses in the process of being used, two shakers of salt and a dish of sliced lemons, the fresh tang of which already pervaded the room. There was also a huge red earthenware dish heaped with thick white biscuits baked in various sizes and shapes, diamonds, hearts, decorated circles and ovals speckled with fruits and spices: the speciality of the fat old witch who, with a veritable army of small dark, darting female skivvies, did the cooking for the establishment.

Jonquil's friend, Don Esteban, entered the room. This was his rancho, his hacienda. He was a small man with narrow olive-skinned features, a thick black moustache drooping over rabbit-teeth and a cast in one eye. He was dressed in a loose-fitting white linen shirt with lace trimmings down the front and tight black-silk pants embroidered on the seams with red flowerlike motifs. A fop he looked, and was. But the boys knew that he was shrewd and cunning and bull-headed also, and here at the rancho his word was absolute law, his people did his every bidding. He spoke directly to Jonquil in Spanish, disdaining to address the bandit-leader's two gringo companions, although, a highly-educated man by border standards he knew their language well. He hated gringos. He couldn't understand why his old compadre, Jonquil, bothered himself with such people.

Jonquil answered briefly and Esteban swung on his heels and left the room.

'All is ready, my friends,' said Jonquil.

Most of the Mexican contingent had been inherited by Esteban from his late uncle, José Lanolito, Jonquil's and Rainey Jay Dodson's old boss, mentor and friend. But Esteban hadn't known Rainey in the old days and didn't want to know him now ...

Esteban was not a *mestizo* like Jonquil; he was pure-bred. Like his uncle, José Lanolito, before him, he was fiercely proud of his Spanish ancestry, jealous of it to the point of madness. He knew Logantown. His hacienda was a far greater place than that ramshackle settlement, his rancho covered more ground. But he knew that, to many of the inhabitants of Logantown he was just another "stinking Mexican". He had known for a long time what he would like to do to Logantown. And he had long coveted the ranches that lay beyond it and from which the town got most of its profits, the grass, the beef. And now here was Jonquil and his friends, who knew more about that territory than Esteban ever would. And Jonquil had a plan.

Esteban hated all Norte-Americanos of whatever stripe or colour. He hated all gringo towns with their false-fronted buildings in the shadows of which gringos lurked. That was all gringos were: false fronts! This town, this gringo place called Logantown, would be put to the sword, the fire. Its men would be slaughtered like the gringo pigs they were, its children would be spitted, its women would be raped and dismembered like swine. The kingdom of Don Esteban and its minions would leave behind a charred waste that other gringos would not forget. And there would be rich pickings.

Much fat beef, horses, assorted livestock. Jonquil could have the money, that was the agreement. Esteban only wanted the stock. And the *revenge!*

CHAPTER 11

It seemed as if they would sweep the town down before them. But, then, even as they almost reached its perimeter, menaced as they were by only sporadic rifle-fire they had a setback. Reinforcements suddenly appeared among the houses and the fire-power became greater. Esteban ordered a retreat, leaving a few of his number motionless or squirming on the ground and sending others, wounded but still partially-mobile to the rear.

In the front of the town Cal Lippton, Jack Trisket, Marshal Crowle and others were congratulating themselves, and each other—not without sardonic undertones from Crowle. He did, however, join with the others in congratulating rancher Rollo Earle and a bunch of his hands who had recently appeared and were enormously welcome.

Rollo said: 'I just recognised somebody out there, Amos, an' I just figured somep'n too. The leader of those hellions now is Don Esteban, the Mex rancher. He hates gringos like poison an' most of all he hates gringo ranchers. The bastard even tried to buy me out once. I think he wants to start a kingdom this side of the border to match the one he's got the other side. Believe me, Amos, that curly wolf ain't here just for the pickings or just to get dinero back for his friend, Jonquil. Esteban loves land and cattle more than anything else, an' he loves power ...'

Rollo was interrupted by Jake Philpott. The young deputy had a shotgun cradled in his good arm. He said; 'They're up to something out there.'

'They could split up,' said Rollo, changing the trend of his conversation. 'They could skirt the town, hit the ranches.'

'I don't think they'd try that,' said Crowle. 'They'd get cut off. They must take the town first. But some of 'em could try skirting the town an' coming in the other way. Like through Mextown for instance.'

'What about Mextown, Amos?'

'Don't worry about Mextown. Mextown has teeth. Whore an' pimps 'ull fight like crazy if their livelihood is threatened, and I don't think the Mexican boys there like Esteban any better than you do, Rollo, huh?'

'No, I guess not.'

'Besides, the Mexican can't afford to split his forces too much.'

And Crowle proved to be right in most, if not all he had said.

Don Esteban's sneak contingent—six picked killers—ran into more than they had bargained for. Two of them were literally hacked to death by the queen-whore herself, Mama Boola and a bevy of her girls. A third was shot fatally in his left eye with a bullet from a derringer in the hand of a pimp called for some obscure reason Johnny Rangatang. Another of Don Esteban's killers received a nasty wound in his thigh from a pitchfork wielded by a Mexican swamper who, under different circumstances the vaquero would have spit upon. This killer and his two compadres retreated pronto, returned to the main force, the wounded one being sent immediately to the rear.

And now Don Esteban flung all his forces into this side of town, aiming to sweep right through to the lusher lands behind, to kill everything in his path on the way through, to leave a clear trail for a return with the spoils he craved. And Jonquil and his friends could take what they sought, the money that they now thought of as theirs by right. Don Esteban had given his word. And, by his lights Don Esteban was an honourable man.

Now pitched battles ensued.

Men fought in gunsmoke and in dust, men on horses, men dismounted. Freight-man Jack Trisket, on foot and bareheaded, a pistol in each hand cut down a screaming Mexican who tried to ride over him. Deputy Jake Philpott, arm in sling blew down a man and horse with one blast of his awkwardly-held but rock-steady shotgun. The huge liveryman, Cal Lippton, his face streaked with blood was down on one knee coolly picking out targets with an army carbine. The pint-sized undertaker, Rab Gray rolled in the dust, the front of his shirt sodden with blood, his face like a ghost's. He became still. Amos Crowle got down on one knee before the body, rose again quickly. Flailing hooves narrowly missed Crowle's head and he grabbed at a stirrup, then a lean tightly-clad leg, feeling the muscles pulse under his hand. A gun went off almost in his face and he felt the searing blast. He yanked hard on the leg and the man came down on top of him.

Crowle used his knee, levering his attacker away from him. He struck out with his gun and felt its barrel jar sickeningly against bone and the Mexican went still. Rising to one knee, Crowle looked about him. Rollo Earle went past, still on horseback. He collided tremendously with a horse and rider from the other side, a huge cloud of dust obscuring them both, the horses' hooves flailing out from the rest of it. The air was full of dust and powder-fumes, making a man cough, his throat and eyes stinging ...

Mayor Kit Blaine sat in a pool of blood, holding his fat stomach, his life running away redly through his pudgy fingers. Old Doc Lessiter lay on his back, his face a red ruin. Crowle's gaze was caught by this sight. There was nothing he could do for Doc, the best friend, except for Deputy Jake that he had had in this stinking town ... A stray bullet hit Crowle's gun. The long-barreled Dragoon Colt was propelled from his hand. He scrabbled for it in the dust and a horse went over him, a swinging hoof grazing his side so that he lay flat for a moment, the sounds of battle going over him and around him. But he got the gun and found it was undamaged and, with it bulking satisfyingly in his hand once more, raised himself on his elbow. An unhorsed Mexican came into his view and he took a shot at the man and missed; the vaquero grabbed a riderless horse and leapt into the saddle and passed on, was lost to Crowle's sight again.

Crowle found himself side by side with the black-moustached saloonkeeper, Jerry Rand who had a blood-dappled hand pressed to his wounded shoulder. But Jerry grinned at the marshal and bent and picked up a pistol from the ground and fired and Crowle saw a man fall, remembering now that he had heard that Jerry was a gunhawk from way back, though their paths had never crossed before. A Mexican rider bore down on them and Crowle raised his own gun and thumbed the hammer. The man was swept away as if by a sudden violent gust of wind and the riderless horse went past.

Crowle suddenly spotted Rainey Jay Dodson.

Then he saw Rainey blown from his horse, though he didn't see which of the townsfolk had fired the shot. The townsfolk were coming up trumps—in spades! He lost sight of Dodson, wondered if he was dead ... A horse went by, its rider's foot caught in the stirrup; the Mexican looked already dead. Crowle lost sight of the saloon-keeper, Jerry Rand. A running man in a big hat came towards Crowle, swinging his rifle by its barrel above his head. Crowle raised his Colt, but now another man got in his way, a youngish townsman he only knew by sight. A knife flashed and the bighatted Mex came to a dead stop. His rifle fell down behind him and he clutched for the sky, the knife protruding from his belly like a strange erect thing. He pitched forward upon it.

'Howdy, marshal,' said the townsman. He bent and rolled the body over and retrieved his knife, wiping it on the dead vaquero's pants.

There were clear places now, less smoke, less dust.

They had had to go; Esteban had had to pull them away. They had had enough, were beginning to feel that the Fates were against them.

And now Esteban began to blame Jonquil, remembering how Jonquil had talked; remembering how Jonquil had *laughed*.

That wild laugh of his. While he talked of a town for the taking and hundreds of head of prime beef.

Esteban had seen very little beef, but he had seen plenty of wild cowboys and wild fighting townsfolk. He had left many of his vaqueros back there on the hard sod and in the scrub-grass on the edges of that Satan-begotten township.

They were going home.

It was full dark now and there was a small breeze, a sliver of moon, a few stars. It could have been a good night. They might have been driving a rich herd. But they had got nothing. Jonquil had got nothing. Don Esteban had a small wound at the back of his neck and his neckerchief chafed it irratingly and he could feel the gummy blood. He halted his men with a furious wave of his hand, pulling himself higher in his saddle as he always did, being a stunted man.

He spoke to Jonquil in their own language.

CHAPTER 12

'He blamed us,' said Jonquil.

They were alone again, the three of them, weary again, thirsty again. Not wealthy either.

'Because me an' him are old compadres,' said Jonquil, 'he let us ride away, he didn't want his hellions tearing us to pieces, he just wanted us gone.' Jonquil started to laugh, but it was a poor effort and not a merry sound.

Fox Raymond said: 'They bulldogged us, that town. Who would've thought it? A stinkin' little town like that!'

Jonquil said: 'The town. And Amos Crowle.'

'Yeh. Black Heart Crowle. Rot his soul.'

'I weel get him,' said Jonquil. 'I swear

to you, amigo, I weell get heem.'

The third member of the party said nothing, and hadn't done so for a long time. Rainey Jay Dodson. He was slumped over a saddle that shone patchily with blood.

'Ain't there a waterhole near here, or a town or somep'n?' said Fox Raymond. 'Some place where we can fill our canteens?'

Now Jonquil seemed to rein in his horse a little, slow down. He seemed hesitant, and it wasn't like him to be hesitant.

'There's Priest's Town.' He waved his hand vaguely over towards the left of them and Fox looked in that direction but couldn't see anything except sand and clumps of scrub-grass and sparse mesquite and other stunted vegetation: even the tough cactus seemed like it had to struggle in this barren stretch. And everything shimmered in a heat-haze that made a man's eyes play him tricks. Jonquil went on: 'It's just a settlement ...'

Fox interrupted him. 'Yeh, you've mentioned it before more'n once. I ain't never bin there. C'mon then. Lead the way, pardner.'

Jonquil said: 'There's only a few dozen people, might be less now. A cluster of hovels, a church with a tall tower.'

'A church?'

'Yes. That's a strange thing. A 'dobe church. But a well-built one. Not a small one. Such a church in such a hole. And the church ees run by a man, half-white, half-Apache, who calls himself Father Peter. The peons are superstitious of him. Even Don Esteban's hellions. He was a friend of my old *jefé*, José Lanolito. I on'y met him once or twice.' Jonquil slapped his hand down on the greasy thigh of his pants with a sound like a pistol-shot. 'Hell, I don't particulary want to get mixed up with that loco ol' coot.'

'Mebbe the old man's daid by now,'

201

said Fox.

Jonquil seemed to brighten a little. 'Yeh!' But then he became morosely silent again as if still unable to make up his mind. And Fox, though still impatient and irritable let things ride for a bit. He didn't want to stir Jonni up into one of his killing rages.

Jonni was unpredictable. Fox didn't question him further. Fox wasn't exactly stupid, however. He might have suspected—he did not *know*—that deep in him Jonni had many of the superstitions of his Indian forebears. He wasn't *all* Mexican. Like a great number of the peons in these parts he was part-Apache.

Maybe he would make up his mind. Maybe he had already done so. Maybe he had a premonition. Maybe he sensed that Priest's Town it would have to be, that that "hole" in the desert was to have a hand in their destiny.

There was sadness in Logantown.

They were burying their dead.

They were burying their enemies too, for they didn't want the town and its environs infested by carrion birds. There wasn't room in the undertaking parlour for all the dead. They had no undertaker either: little Rab Gray had died in the battle. The grisly jobs were done quickly by volunteers. The words would have to wait.

A grim-faced Marshal Crowle was interrogating a wounded prisoner, and he wasn't being gentle about it. The man slumped on a bench in the law-office. He had been shot in the leg and was holding a kerchief to the wound to staunch the blood. Crowle was reminded that the town had no medico now, that his good friend, Doc Lessiter had been among the fatalities. The prisoner was tough. But he was scared. He was one of Don Esteban's vaqueros, a mestizo who had very little English. Crowle had some Spanish. But the man's replies were garbled. He was torn between fear of Crowle and an almost superstitious dread of his *jefé,* Don Esteban, even though the Don was long gone and it didn't seem likely he would return. The vaquero, Crowle opined, was a pretty stupid son of a bitch. He had no time to waste. He told Jake to get jailbird Juan out of the cell. And Juan did some translating. The upshot of it all was that, not long after Juan had put in his two cents' worth he and Crowle left town together.

Juan, of course, had no gun, had no weapon of any kind. Crowle had his long-barreled hand-gun, a Winchester rifle in its saddle-boot and enough assorted ammunition to take on an army, though he didn't figure he'd have to do anything like that. Back in town Juan had with very little prompting told the vaquero just what *Senor Black Heart* would do to him if he didn't answer questions properly—and *pronto.*

Not that, in the long run the man had much to tell. But, it had been pretty obvious even to a *stupido* like him that there was a falling-pit between gangleader Jonquil and Don Esteban. Things certainly hadn't happened the way Jonquil had promised.

And now maybe Don Esteban would peg Jonquil and his friends out in the desert to die.

Then again—and this was Juan's opinion—maybe the Don would just part company with Jonquil forever. The Don had a sense of honour and Jonquil was, after all an old compadre: they had fought side by side in the past.

One way or another, Amos Crowle had to find out ...

They passed the area of Buzzard's Point and Crowle remembered how he himself had been staked out here to die not so long ago and had been saved by a fancy young gink called Rainey Jay Dodson. Such a lot had happened since then and now here he was on a killing trail after that same Rainey. If Rainey was still alive that is, Crowle thought: he had seen the younker get hit. There were no bodies under the sun at Buzzard's Point now. They went on, Juan riding a little ahead of Crowle all the time as he had been ordered to do. Juan, not wanting his head blown off, was being a very good boy. But, as Crowle had barely laid a finger on him so far maybe Juan was getting his confidence back, and the marshal was taking no chances.

The marshal had promised Juan his life.

But could Juan trust such a black-hearted one?

Juan played along. He took the marshal first to the hideout. It was empty, didn't look as if it had been visited lately.

Juan was of the opinion that if Jonni and his friends were separated from the main party they would have gone to Priest's Town. Juan knew Priest's Town. He didn't like it. He didn't think Jonni liked it much either. But that would be the place, Juan thought.

Jonquil had made up his mind.

Here was a town they *could* take. A town on which they could work off their spleen. A town which they could use in any form they wanted, in any ways their evil and cantankerous minds could devise.

This was a peaceful town, a town where simple peons tilled the meagre soil from dawn to dusk and then slept in their hovels with their dogs and their fowl and, if they were lucky, a horse or two. Just a dozen souls or so, old and young, inter-bred, timid, superstitious. They had heard of Jonquil, as who hadn't in the borderlands? A couple of them at least whispered among themselves that once they had actually *seen* him. And when this big man with the cruel grin and the maniac laugh appeared in the town at last, it was as if the devil himself had descended upon them. Most of them fled, taking their women and children with them. One man was shot because he feebly tried to defend his wife and his two grown daughters. Theirs was the biggest house and the only one in the settlement that was completely constructed of logs. The older woman was set to help Rainey Dodson, who was pretty bad. The two girls were put to prepare food under the watchful eye of Fox Raymond. They were on a good thing here, thought the small redbearded outlaw. Food, a bed, young well-fleshed girls.

Fox was outside watching one girl at the pump, admiring her shape, when Father Peter appeared. Fox took a shot at him. The father retreated into his church and Jonquil came running out of the cabin.

'Goddam whitehaired ol' feller in long black skirts,' said Fox.

Jonquil said: 'So he ees still alive.'

Fox said: 'Mebbe I nicked him. But I didn't slow him down.' He laughed nastily. 'He ran like a goddam jackrabbit.'

'It's bad luck to shoot a priest.'

'Horse-shit,' said Fox.

Jonquil's eyes flared for a moment and then the flame died. He said: 'We'll take a look over there. Go tell Rainey where we're going.'

'An' old priest ain't gonna do us any harm,' grumbled Fox. But he went to do Jonquil's bidding. Nothing had worked out the way Fox had figured. He wasn't a rich man the way he had planned to be. He was as bare-assed as a wandering waddy.

Fox thought Rainey might just pull through—if that fat old sow in the cabin pulled off a miracle or something. Rainey's chest had been shredded by a shotgun blast and it was in fact a plumb miracle that he was still alive. Fox spat at the Mexican corpse outside the door of the cabin. Then he went in and told Rainey what was what and stroked a plump young female buttock in passing and then returned to Jonquil and said:

'Rainey didn't seem interested.' He

chuckled. And Jonquil said: 'Help me drag that carcase to the church.'

'You gonna say a few words over him, Jonni?'

The big man didn't bother to reply to this witticism. Fox went on. 'I hope that preacher ain't got a scatter-gun or somep'n.'

'That ain't likely. He's a man of peace.'

Fox said: 'That place is like a goddam fortress.' But he got hold of one leg of the corpse while Jonquil grasped the other and they dragged the light burden across the sod, raising puffs of dust. A little yellow dog came yelping from cover and Jonquil gave him a glancing kick and he fled with clamorous indignation. The church was silent. Nothing moved now anywhere near the grim and ludicrous cortege. The peons had fled to the meagre fields or further, to the desert even. The church was a strange thing to find in such a piteous place. It was of thick adobe and had a tall square tower. Its windows were high, its steps wide, its long double-doors stout and imposing. The doors were closed and looked impregnable. The windows were black, blank, sightless.

Jonquil said: 'It's said that Father Peter built this place himself when he first came here as a young man.'

'He must've had some help,' said Fox sardonically.

'I think it's older than that. But why ...?' Jonquil's voice tailed off.

They left the body at the bottom of the steps and Jonquil climbed the steps and tried the door. He pushed against it. It didn't budge. He returned to Fox and said: 'I reckon eet is barred inside. Better take a look around I suppose, amigo. Maybe the priest's got somebody hiding in there.'

It hardly seemed likely, thought Fox, but he went along. They skirted the church. Nothing moved, human or animal. There was a narrow back door, but this was of log too and seemed impregnable. They went round the front again, passing the corpse. 'Didn't want him stinkin' up the place where we were,' said Jonquil unnecessarily. Then, irrelevantly: 'We'll need extra mounts I guess, just in case.'

They found one single spavined beast refreshing itself at a chipped and leaning adobe horse-trough.

Fox said: 'They must've took the others with 'em.'

Jonquil said: 'What others?'

The question was unanswerable. From where they stood they could see right through the single main street, if it could be called that, with ramshackle edifices straggled each side of it. Nothing moved at either end and one vista was as depressing as the other. They might have been at the ass-end of Creation.

They were walking again towards the log cabin with Fox trailing the slow docile old horse with a short length of rope that was around its neck when the bells began to ring.

Bells from the grey, square church tower.

The sound was like that of a huge copper ball rolling along the dusty street of the empty town, resounding; sounding out into the open lands around and awakening strange echoes in this town, empty except for the little old priest who tolled the bells, the two *whole* killers and the damaged one, the fat woman and her two nubile daughters.

Fox Raymond clapped his hands to his ears. 'Godamighty! That crazy old bastard!'

His companion jeered: 'Try an' stop him then.' And he marched on towards the cabin. Fox stood irresolute for a moment, pouring curses at Jonquil's broad back, but not too loudly. Then he went back to the church and climbed the steps. Flies were already clustered over the body of the peon and buzzed angrily as Fox passed them. He tried the door, charged it, kicked it. He took out his gun and hammered on the stout wood with the butt. The bells rang above him like doom, tolling with a steady, melancholy rhythm. Fox began to yell, but his voice was a thin thing against the voice of the bells.

He began to prowl around the church. The windows were high up; he could only reach them if he stood on something and he couldn't see anything on which to climb. He reached the back door and put a few bullets into it, hoping to smash the lock. He made no impression. Anyway, he thought, the door was probably barred on the inside. He felt as if he would like to keep on firing the gun, however, because it helped to kill the sound of the bells. If only he could actually *kill* those bells!

He reloaded. He went back around the church. He did not fire the gun again. Jonquil came running from the cabin, waving his arms, screaming, 'What in hell's the matter with you?'

Fox said: 'I was jus' trying to blow the back door in, that's all, Jonni. No good. But if I could find somep'n to climb on I could mebbe get through a window.'

'Yeh, an' mebbe break a leg.' Jonquil grinned, his good humour restored for a bit. 'Let that loco ol' coyote get on with it. Come back here. I want you to keep watch.'

Fox kept watch. And, standing opposite the church as he was the bells seemed to be coming right at him, gonging inside his skull. He told himself that they were just bells, that was all. Jeeze, he thought, that old man must be tireless, he doesn't miss a beat! Fox's head began to thud, to vibrate. He spat. Hell, he couldn't even spit properly! Only a maniac would want to spend his life in this dry waste. 'One of us ought to go an' shoot that ol' buzzard,' he said aloud, stupidly.

Jonquil heard him and said: 'You know how to get at him, huh?'

'You know I don't.'

Jonquil said: 'Why's he doing it?' He seemed to be asking himself the question. But Fox tried to answer it. 'I guess he just wants to get on our nerves. Don't let it get to yuh, boy.' He laughed inanely. But it was getting to *him*. Jonquil didn't say anything else, went back into the cabin. He had figured he would have himself a time with one of the girls. But all he did was curl up in a corner and fall into an uneasy slumber, trying to make up for the long sleepless ride through the night. But the bells were now sounding in his head like the beat of doom and, underneath their sound were the other sounds that came from Rainey Dodson lying on the dirty cot in the corner. The wet, bubbling sounds.

We ought to get out of here, thought Jonquil. But he did not bestir himself.

The bells went on and, outside Fox Raymond began to pace fretfully back and forth. Nobody can stop the bells he thought, the devil himself can't stop the bells. 216

EPILOGUE

They were puzzled when they first heard the bells, but they were following the trail now and the trail went that way, the hoofmarks, and Juan said this was the way to Priest's Town.

The bells lead them more quickly to the town, if it could be called a town.

They idled their horses and looked at the quiet, sprawling, dingy settlement ahead of them. Nothing moved. 'Yes, eet ees Priest's Town,' Juan said. They were side by side now almost as if they were compadres.

Crowle raised himself in his stirrups and shaded his eyes with his hand. There might be men watching. He thought they were probably out of rifle-range. But distances were deceptive in this flat hot land.

For a moment—and probably for the first time during the long ride—the marshal's attention was diverted from his prisoner, his guide. And Juan did something that was completely unexpected; *completely,* it seemed, out of character.

He seized his opportunity. He reached out with a hand and pushed the other man. Then he put spurs to his horse, the startled beast bounding forward. Crowle reeled in the saddle but did not tumble from it. He straightened. He drew his hand-gun, raised it, steadied it with his other hand beneath his wrist. 'Hold up, you fool!' he yelled. But Juan and the horse went on, if somewhat erratically, drawing out of range. Crowle knew he could make it with a rifle. He lowered the Colt, however, and he did not draw the rifle. He chuckled. 'You've had your chance, brother,' he said softly, aloud. He holstered the gun. He set his horse at a gallop.

Rainey Jay Dodson lay on his cot in the dusky corner. He did not know where the women had gone, or his friends. Maybe they had all gone, left him here. He wished he could join his friends with the women. The cabin-door was slightly open and a spear of sun came through. More jagged splinters of sunlight had found their way through the interstices in the worn sacking over the single window. But Rainey's eyes were playing him tricks and the light danced and fluctuated and now and then almost faded completely like flames dying. The big Mexican woman had bound his wounds. She hadn't been clean and the rags she had used hadn't been clean. But she had used some herb salve too, or some such home remedy. He wasn't feeling much pain now, just a sort of dullness.

He had heard the bells. The bells were still going on.

The door swung a little wider but

nobody came in. The wind? ...

The bells ... Then he thought he heard somebody shout; it sounded like 'They're coming'. Who's coming, Rainey thought? Amos Crowle? A posse? Goddamit he thought, where's my gun? He felt naked without his gun.

It lay, belt and all on a packing case behind his head.

As he twisted himself around the pain began to tear at him again with redhot steel claws. But his hand closed around the butt of the gun and he drew it slowly from its holster and the feel of it was very satisfying.

Somehow, he managed to get off the cot. Gun in hand, he dragged himself across to the door. Manoeuvring himself around the jamb, he got himself into a sitting position. He sat, trying to lift the gun.

The pain beat at him in cruel waves. I don't think I can stand anymore, he thought.

And the pain went away. And even

the sound of the bells faded ...

Juan had reached the town without being shot down by one of his friends. And now Juan had a gun. One thing about the gang, they always carried some spare armoury.

The second horseman came straight as an arrow for the single main street of the town. He was plastered low to his horse's neck and only his legs could be seen.

Juan had a vantage point on the steps of the church. The bells dinned in his ears. But he hadn't had so much of them as the other two had. Fox Raymond and Jonquil stood in the centre of the dusty street with their guns ready. Jonquil had two Colt forty-fives. Fox had a big Navy hand-gun and a Henry rifle. He holstered the hand-gun and lifted the rifle to his shoulder and levelled it, squinting against the sun. Crowle had the sun in his favour. But then, suddenly, the horse and rider were no longer there. At the last minute, Crowle had veered off the trail. The sound of the bells killed the hoofbeats.

As, rifle raised Fox turned full around the man on foot appeared at the other end of the street. Fox took a shot at him, the rifle still not quite at his shoulder, a snapshot; the man disappeared and Fox knew he hadn't hit him. Both Jonquil and Juan were facing back that way now also, but there was nothing they could shoot at. The bells went on like a brassy chorus. 'There!' yelled Fox Raymond suddenly, though the others didn't hear him, only saw his strained and open mouth. This time he raised his rifle completely to his shoulder and tried to cover the moving figure.

Even as he fired he was recoiling from the bullet that smashed into his chest and his rifle-fire was like a flat echo of the rolling report of Crowle's Colt. Fox's rifle-slug whined away into the air, the sound lost in the sound of the bells. Fox hit the dust hard with his back and his toes kicked up and he became still. Half-crouching, one on the church-steps, one in the street, Juan and Jonquil triggered their weapons. But again there was nothing to shoot at. Jonquil ran. Juan followed his old *jefé*. They found partial cover in a small stable. The bells had rung without a break while the gunfire sounded, and now the bells went on, the only sound now, killing all smaller ones.

And Amos Crowle might be creeping up, unheard, unseen. All Juan's superstitious fears of the man were back. *The blackhearted one.* Now Juan wished ... 'Cover me,' snarled Jonquil in Juan's ear, making him jump.

Jonquil ran out of the stable, turned sharply and dived headfirst through the door of the cabin where the three women had been, where a grinning *unmoving* Rainey Jay Dodson now guarded the portals.

Jonni's loco, thought Juan, he always

has been. Jonni and Crowle: two maniacs! Juan wished he could get out of there and leave them to it. If he could get to his horse ... He moved to the doorway of the stable.

Amos Crowle stood on the steps of the church near to the body of the dead peon. He fired two shots but Juan didn't hear the reports because of the bells. He felt as if he was kicked twice; powerful hooves smashed him backwards, stamped him into the hard ground. He struggled feebly; but then he cried out once, a high, thin despairing sound, and he curled up, holding himself; and so he died. A life had been promised. A life had been taken .. Jonquil appeared in the doorway of the log cabin and Crowle flung himself forward and down and the shots went above him. Then, from his prone position Crowle triggered two shots off also. Jonquil went back into the black hole of the doorway again. There was another figure there, seated on the ground; but it wasn't moving.

Crowle rose and flung himself at a tangent. Bullets spat around him. He didn't go for the doorway but for the sacking-covered window. He went through it in a sort of crablike motion but lifting himself as no crab could. Jonquil had gone through the back. There was a lot of blood around, though obviously not all of it was Jonquil's, maybe none of it at all. Had he pulled out because he was hit or was he just making a strategic retreat? Now it was Crowle's turn to retreat. Rainey Jay Dodson sat in the doorway and grinned a death's grin at his old sparring partner, Amos. His gun was in his lap. He looked as if he had died mighty hard. Crowle took the gun and wiped the blood from it. Maybe he'd need an extra gun.

His next stop was at the stable where Juan's body lay. He went down on one knee, lifted a loose board and peered out. He could not see Jonquil. He went out again and round and it was then that Jonquil opened up from cover somewhere to the left of him. But Crowle was moving quickly and the range was fairly long. Wounded or not, Jonquil had moved pretty fast. One bullet took Crowle's hat off, the other missed him but by no great margin. The Mexican leader was still a shooting fool! Crowle reached the shelter of a nearby privy. Jonquil was out of sight; there was not even an arm or a leg showing. The echoes of the shots had died and the bells still rang, tirelessly and, suddenly Amos Crowle felt the sheer uncanniness of it all. It was as if the bells were being manipulated by a ghostly hand tolling a knell for the dead.

He shook his fancies away; the bells might din in his ears, but they did nothing for his nose, and the stench in this tumbledown privy was enough to make a man gag. People who lived in places like this usually shat in the open, he thought. So maybe this leaning edifice was by way of being a one-upper on the neighbours. A few yards ahead was another pile of timber that might have once been a pigsty, but, *whatever,* Crowle figured it couldn't possibly stink worse than the privy. Weaving, he ran for it. Shots blasted so quickly that Jonquil must have been fanning the hammer of his gun. Once more—for he had picked it up once—Crowle lost his hat. It was obtaining more perforations than a frypan at a shooting match. He reached his new cover, but it was little more useful than a dancing whore's G-string. Wood was chewed and holed and chips showered Crowle. He caught a glimpse of Jonquil. He was in a small hut made of adobe and sacking. Crowle let off a couple of shots and Jonquil's head bobbed down like that of a turkey at a shoot. Crowle checked both his guns quickly, replenished their load with shells from his belt.

As he did so, he moved backwards, keeping the crumbling shelter between him and the big Mexican, hoping to move around, maybe flank the man. But almost as if divining his adversary's intention, Jonquil moved too, crablike and Crowle caught a fleeting glimpse of part of the big man's anatomy and took a shot at it and missed. The bullet hit something metallic, maybe a nail-head, and ricocheted, whined away. But it must have been close; Jonquil rolled, scrabbled. Like a big animal. He went out of sight behind a pile of rubbish then appeared again like a gopher out of a hole. Crowle took another shot at him.

Jonquil missed a beat but then went on again. Now he seemed to be dragging his one leg. He went behind the shelter of another small adobe hut. The gunfire had stopped again. There was only the bells. Crowle ran, recklessly. But weaving. He dived headfirst through a narrow doorway and rolled. No slugs blasted at him. He went right through the hovel and he was on the street. A fat Mexican woman went by, helped by two comely girls, probably her daughters, he thought. They all screamed when they saw him and they hurried their pace; the old lady was dragged along as more shots blasted past them now.

Jonquil was on the other side of the street, half-crouching in the meagre cover of a horse-trough. His eyes seemed to be glaring and his white teeth were bared.

He had lost his hat and the white slash across his black hair was prominent, gleaming under the sun. The bells rang. They seemed very clear out here, pure-toned.

Jonquil yelled something. Then he started to laugh, leaning forward over the horse-trough, propping himself, a gun the extension of his long arm, the black muzzle pointing at Crowle.

Crowle took time, if only an in-finitesmal fragment of it.

He was orientated quicker. He was

faster. He squeezed off his first shot.

Jonquil was thrown backwards by the tearing power of the heavy bullet.

His mouth was still open, his teeth bared in a wide grin. As if he were still laughing. But now, after the shot there didn't seem to be any other sound above the bells.

Jonquil didn't fall all the way backwards, but teetered, while Crowle watched, his gun levelled, waited. And Jonquil dropped his gun in the horse-trough with a small splash: Crowle saw the water rise a little. Then Jonquil clawed for something with his big, empty hands and found nothing and pitched forward and landed almost neatly in the horse-trough.

Fountains of water rose now. Crowle lowered his gun, needing no second shot. Water slopped onto the parched ground.

Striding forward, Crowle realised that the bells had at last stopped ringing. Everything was still now. Jonquil's legs

230

stuck up out of the horse-trough, but it was deep and the rest of him was submerged. His riding boots were badly scuffed. His spurs gleamed in the sunlight.

The blood came up through the murky water, swirled, made pink, shifting patterns. Crowle turned back, went to retrieve his hat.

When he returned there was a small, black-clad figure on the steps of the church beside the body of the peon. And the women were going there.

As the three women, the older one and the two young nubile ones approached the little priest and the corpse on the steps they began to wail.

The people began to appear like grey ghosts on the plain and move slowly to the town.